MW00460343

CHINESE NEW YEAR

BY C.E. O'BANION

TEXAS BOOK PUBLISHERS ASSOCIATION

HOUSTON TEXAS

CHINESE NEW YEAR

C.E. O'BANION

TEXAS BOOK PUBLISHERS ASSOCIATION
HOUSTON TEXAS

WWW.TEXASBOOKPUBLISERS.ORG

Copyright © 2021 by C.E. O'Banion
All rights reserved

First Edition

13 12 11 10 9 8 7 6 5 4 3 2 1

ISBN 978-1-946182-29-6 (hard back)
ISBN 978-1-946182-30-2 (trade paper)
ISBN 978-1-946182-31-9 (ePub)

Book and cover design by
Brian Callaghan
Richmond, VA
https://hokiecal-art.myshopify.com

Map on page 31 created by
Kim Howard
Baton Rouge, LA

This is a work of fiction. Names, characters, business, events and incidents are the products of the author's imagination. Any resemblance to actual persons, living or dead, or actual events is purely coincidental.

TEXAS BOOK PUBLISHERS ASSOCIATION
www.texasbookpublishers.org

HOUSTON TEXAS

Dedicated To

Mel, Flan, H.D., E.Z. and my friend, Tapscott

CHAPTER 1

His folding walker gleamed in the early-summer sun, the cabernet-colored aluminum slick from the draped humidity. It was 8:09 in the morning in Baton Rouge, Louisiana, and Alton B. Tapscott was late.

His calloused brow showed his years of hard-scrabble work in the state-funded education sector—some leathered skin appeared so tough you couldn't cut it with a Texas chainsaw, while patches were bruised or translucent like he'd gotten a skin-graft from a toad. His voluminous khaki pants and long sleeve, brown corduroy shirt gave him the look of an aging safari guide. The outfit, pulled from his closet of earth tones and muted outerwear he deemed sensible and complimentary to his shape, bunched at the inner thighs and belly then swelled out as if suffering from a peanut allergy. The sleeves protected him from the roving gangs of mosquitos and gnats that corrupted this otherwise harmless stretch of city block, and the pants hid an embarrassing scar from a botched knee surgery decades before, when he tore a ligament genuflecting during mass. It was his second-to-last time in a house of worship. He elected to skip the calisthenics for his wife's funeral two years ago.

His pants were patched in the crotch numerous times, usually with whatever mismatching fabric the women at Tin's Tailoring shop on the street corner had lying around. "More yard work," he muttered loud enough for them to hear when dropping off each pair of pleats, either in khaki, olive, or navy. "Tore them pulling weeds!"

He loathed the color black—despite its capacity to slim—and refused to allow even a pinstripe that would attract that kind of heat. The holes in the pants were not from laborious feats, but from the years of aggressive sitting of an avid indoorsman and even more aggressive stubbornness to avoid shopping at the mall.

Big box brands' fashion departments hadn't yet caught up to Mr. Tapscott's unique shape. Thoreau, which he often attempted to quote, once said to never trust a job that requires new clothes, but Thoreau lived in a cabin and Alton Tapscott had access to delivery pizza which necessitated a wardrobe evolution before a résumé update. Years of online shopping and online returning made shoe buying a chore he wished to avoid, so he had a reasonable pair of tanned leather sandals encasing his eggshell-white, prescription, compression, tube socks. The German sandals were the one luxury item Mr. Tapscott afforded himself, and he insisted his old friend and attorney, Charles Logan, include them in his latest will. They would go to the delivery boy from Zippy's Mexican Cantina.

Baton Rouge, Louisiana, as described by Tapscott upon his family's move there years before, was the tuna fish salad sandwich of American quasi-metropolises. One might not regale a stranger with tales of lukewarm, processed seafood and mayonnaise glory, the same as many never thought to mention Louisiana's capital city in comparison to its more visited and defecated-upon staple to the south, New Orleans. It's imperative to understand the difference between tuna salad and tuna steak, he'd continue—the steak was a cut of meat from a large mackerel. They could live up to fifty years. You caught one of these giants and pulled him onto the boat you were renting for a relative's sixtieth birthday, had your guide cut him into pieces that he told you were edible, and you had a fancy feast. Tuna salad wasn't as much a precise cut as it was an array of chunks and hunks, pulled off the fish in a hurry and spilled out of a can … it could last for well over fifty years.

If the town was a tuna fish sandwich, the heat was the mayonnaise, liberally spread, the celery the delicious smell of appropriated New Orleans' culture, and the tuna was, well, the seafood. The seafood was done well, mostly, which added to the distinct smell about the place: A homogenous waft of fried seafood and chemical refineries that reeked of a posthumous carnival or, as Tapscott referred to it, like sticking your head into one of those old McDonald's indoor playground's plastic slides and taking a gulp of air up your nose. It was as hot in Baton Rouge as it was everywhere in the northern hemisphere, but a summer breeze in Louisiana best compared to the stifling puff of a diesel exhaust. The heat paired well with the daily three o'clock rain shower, sweeping over the tops of magnolias before evaporating on beds of roots carpeting the ground, themselves retreating deeper and deeper into the dirt these last few years. The city itself prioritized air flow over conditioning—the cancer rate was high from the nearby refineries—but few rooms went without a ceiling fan, and for those that did, Tapscott chose to travel with a small box fan.

The rush of the Mississippi River tore a path through town, carving out a seam on the west side like an ice cream scooper, separating Baton Rouge from the western continental territories except for a system of haphazard bridges and ferries. Down the slopes of the river's levy, and beyond a two mile stretch of clapboard houses the color of jellybeans clinging to the side of the road that Tapscott's neighbor once called "fruit town," sat the Garden District. There, the creaky houses loomed over the overgrown sidewalks, their Victorian, Spanish, or Tudor facades shaded by the umbrella of oak trees lining each street's median. The streets were all named after wisteria, gardenias, or olives and oleanders, except for one: Eugene St.

Where he waited.

Mr. Tapscott's son, Archie, called a driver for him after the old wagon failed industry standards years prior and was labeled unsafe for human transportation. He'd accosted the portly woman at the Kwik Kar Inspection and Haircut Depot near the bank of the Mississippi River's levy with a barrage of customary promises to get the four lights on the dash looked at soon enough, but it didn't work, and his once-proud green wagon sat idle in the car port.

It was 8:12. The whirring click of cicadas moved the air, rumbling the branches around him. Their droll consistency scared Tapscott sometimes, like his across-the-street neighbor that mowed his lawn at seven in the morning every Monday and Friday.

His pocket, wrist, and ear buzzed as a soft, comfortable female voice echoed throughout his head.

"New message from Archer Tapscott. Interested?"

"Interested!" he said, standing at attention, alone on the street corner. "Interested!"

"Read, delete, or—"

"Read! Read!"

The voice changed to his son's when the message swept through his auditory canals.

"Hey, Dad."

"Dammit," Alton said to the bustling family of squirrels trolling across the powerlines connecting Eugene and Tulip streets. The lines snaked from house to house, vines of industry, pumping each living room with just enough air and television to make it livable.

The soothing voice responded, *"Reply with 'Dammit!' Yes or—"*

"No! No!" Another squirrel scurried up a nearby crape myrtle, struggling up the leafy, slender branches until the tops bent over and around the strong neck of a Tudor's brick chimney.

"Reply with a message, Alton?"

"Yes. And don't call me Alton." Remembering he was in public, and speaking to one of his closest companions, he put on a smile and sounded as a mother of four might when speaking to a teenaged waiter. "Please, LIZA," he said through gritted teeth.

"*I understand, Mister Tapscott. Would you like to reply with a message ... Mister Tapscott?*"

"Yes." He was still smiling in the direction of a passing cloud. "Tell my son the car hasn't arrived. Ask him where the car is. I'm late."

After a short time, LIZA responded, "*Here is your pending message, Mister Tapscott: Tell my son, Archie, the car hasn't arrived. Ask him where the car is. I'm late.*"

"LIZAAAA." He made sure to smile as a car swept by, a bag flying through the passenger window, sending aluminum cans clunking across the pavement. "Translate to the first person, please, ma'am."

"Okay, Mister Tapscott. Your message is: 'The car isn't here, my son, Archie. And I don't know where it is, but I'm late.' Confirm?"

"Yes. Send."

"*Confirm?*"

"Yes. Send message."

"*Do you confirm, Mister Tapscott?*"

"Confirm! Shit!"

"*Okay, Mister Tapscott. You have confirmed the message. Now do you want to send, delete, or hold for—*"

"Send! Send! Send!"

"*Thank you, Mister Tapscott. Three messages sent to Archer Tapscott.*"

Alton looked toward the cloud and grit his teeth, and,

following Dr. Addison's guidance on misplaced hostility, screamed, "Merry Christmas!" It wasn't Christmas, but the Verba-LIZA 6.0 was a Yuletide tiding from Archie a year before. A sleek model of cochlear implants that aid the elderly in communication and cognitive connections, as ran the ad campaign. The promise of less predictive text, the ever-more out-of-focus keys, and an interactive female voice, convinced him to give it a try. The AMBER alerts from Tangipahoa Parish proved to be a new-age lobotomy.

His eyes caught the blunt glint of an old, black sedan rounding the corner. Archie told him the car would be Midnight Black, but LIZA never explained what that meant—she only pulled up different dark images on his computer's screen.

As the car approached, a flurry of stickers across the side of the vehicle came into view: the driver's preferred political party, operating system, social media, and something about their pet's social worth. He gave a sharp grunt as each sticker came into focus.

At some point, around 2020, he decided politics were for the birds, and he certainly couldn't stomach what he referenced as the abhorrent, hostile overtaking of corporate cookie cutter advertisers from the real creatives of his day, the last stronghold of artists: the cereal box slogan writers. No, the country was rotting from the inside, had been since it was founded, and politicians were nothing more than pirates quarrelling over the scraps of a once great bounty.

That year he'd stood triumphantly at the doors of a gymnasium on the north end of town, shaking his head at the throngs of American flag clad voters in line through the morning hours. His wife dragged him out of bed for the occasion, sensing a lull in their civic performance as of late. Groups wore shirts with the phrase "TAKE IT BACK" scrawled across the front and "NEVER AGAIN!" on the backside.

"If only they knew they'd be doing this again in four years," he whispered to Mel. If only they knew he'd thrown his vote away on the Green Party, their fury would be like a bath. He'd pulled back the curtain to the voting booth around the gym's 3-point line, took a step toward the electronic voting machine, and waited. He waited for what he thought was a necessary amount of time, banged his hand on the computer, as if voting was an activity that required a certain amount of noise, and walked back out. He got a little sticker that said, "I voted!" and an enthusiastic high-five from another white man at the front of the line. "Who'd you pick?" he'd asked Mel, who stood perturbed on the cusp of the bleacher steps. "Oh, not him, right? Her?!"

*****

The window rolled down, and the roar of the air conditioner shook a few blue spotted cotingas, migrants from the increasingly present tropic, from their limbs. Alton saw a pair of sunken green eyes behind thick, gold- rimmed eyeglasses that transitioned from clear to shade as the sun splashed in through the lowered window. "You Mister Tap-scott? Alton?"

"That I am. And *you're* late," Tapscott said.

The driver fell into his horn, laughing. "Okay, good one. Sorry about being late, but, hey, I'm here now. And you know I don't really control this thing."

"So why am I paying you and not the car?"

"That's a good question. That's a real good question!" the driver said, "But, hey, I gotta eat, right?"

"I suppose," he replied, inching over the scorched grass blades toward the curb's precipice.

"Need some help?" the driver asked.

Tapscott heard him fiddling with the door handle.

"Stay in your car! Stay … in … your … car." It was enough of an obstacle this early in the morning, but to talk while descending the curb might've overwhelmed Alton if not for the sheer embarrassment of masculine vulnerability that put a fragment of pep in his sandal soles.

"You got it?"

"I got it. I got it. It's these damn sandals." He hopped down onto the pavement. "They were made for more social affairs. Not outdoor recreation."

"Okay. Well, let's get to … 225 Park Boulevard?"

Alton was perplexed by the lack of punctuality and the question. "Are you asking me? Don't you know the way? If you don't, won't this thing?" Alton waved one hand at the car.

"Just confirming, Mr. Tapscott."

"Confirm!"

Tapscott descended into the backseat of the car, a process he'd mastered over the years. He swiveled on each heel until his backside faced the open car door, then fell into the pleather seat. The walker dissembled, folding at the patented four joint buckling system with the click of a button, just like the salesman said it would. Like an arthritic acrobat, he was learned in the art of intermittent bursts of energy followed by controlled breathing.

"Water? Gum?" The customary ride-share *mise en place* Tapscott was used to.

"Just a ride, thanks. And more A/C if this thing has the goose-power."

"Oh, it's got the goose-power." The driver smiled, revealing a row of almost blinding white teeth, and he turned a large dial to the right as a small snowflake burned blue on the dashboard.

The automobile: on the one hand the sputtering, screeching, spitting, smog, sirens, and traffic, not to mention exponential increase in loss of human life from almost any aspect of its origin; on the other hand, one of the few times a human can feel like a refrigerated food product through advancements in A/C.

Tapscott felt the cooling power of what he assumed was an older model Subaru Outback—a car advertisers lined up for a rebrand sometime around 2039 when the Outback was deemed too harsh a reminder for selling purposes. A sensible buy, nonetheless.

"Tap-scott," the driver said, emphasizing each syllable. "Is that Scottish?"

"I would have no way of knowing. Probably American," he replied.

The driver let the word roll over his tongue a few more times. "Tap ... Scott. Tap ... Scott." Then said it twice, fast enough for his tongue to get lost. "You just don't hear a name like that often. Down here at least. Are you from down here?"

"As much as the next guy," Tapscott said.

"Didn't wanna sit up front, huh? No problem, no problem. I understand. Been driving for too long not to understand. You're gonna need to buckle up before the car lets me go anywhere though." The cheerful attitude of the driver and the minor inconvenience of putting on a seatbelt caused an involuntary clinch of Alton's eyelids. Riding in the back allowed him to feel he was wealthier than if he were riding shotgun like a kid on the way to laser tag.

"My name is not late, by the way. It's Sikander." He extended a dark bronzed arm up to his rearview mirror and turned it until Alton sat square in the frame.

Alton noticed a button out of place on his shirt and adjusted, glancing back to see Sikander's eyes still on him.

"You aren't hot in that get-up?"

"I long for the days of just hot," Tapscott said. "But I'd as soon die of heat stroke as I would be eaten alive by these skeeter hawks passing along whatever disease they've conjured up in some shrunken bayou around here."

"People say it's getting hotter out there every day, but I don't really see it. However, I guess you can't really see heat, so maybe that's a good thing, huh? At least, I heard that on the news."

"I guess you've never been to New Mexico," Tapscott said.

"I actually have. Twice. But it was to ski, so it was decades ago."

Tapscott opened one wrinkled eyelid to study his chauffeur's age. He'd have guessed the boy a greenhorn of sorts. His unwrinkled, yellow shirt shone in the shade of the cabin. Tapscott always wondered how people went about wearing clothes all day and not picking up a wrinkle along the way. He guessed maybe thirty-three, but that would've put him at three or four a couple of decades ago. Surely not in ski-school age. Rather than ask, he concluded Sikander was either a winter sports phenom driving a shuttle service for extra money or a liar. Baton Rouge was a peculiar offseason destination for a man about the mountain, so he concluded a liar.

"Skiing? Really? I prefer to vacation on vacation. Always felt a bit busy, zooming about this way and that."

Sikander turned his slim shoulders to face Tapscott. "Oh, it was wonderful."

Tapscott snapped his eye shut, waiting for Sikander to turn around.

"I was young, but you bet I kicked some ass out there! Yep!"

"Okay, okay." Tapscott waved his left hand like he was breaking up a smoke ring. "We appear to have gotten too excited. Eyes on the road, please."

"But I don't need—"

"It makes me feel better if *someone* is watching other than a satellite," Alton said. "And maybe if my tip is good enough, we can get you up to Arkansas or Alaska for some of your precious skiing. Somewhere up north, I guess." Alton again gestured with his left hand, flinging it up north, eyes closed. Always considering anything north of Dallas to be "up there," Tapscott assumed it snowed year-round most places.

He let his head sink into the rest and his mind wander. *Skiing*, he thought, smiling. *What a fruitless endeavor. No money in it.*

"So, what do you do for work, Mr. Tap-scott?"

His eyes shot open, staring at the putty-colored ceiling of the Midnight Black sedan. "I'm retired. Was a professor. Of ... literature."

He realized now they were driving down the same street he'd taken to work, and he began to spot the new build homes sprouting from the oak root splintered lawns. Branches were piled on the street's edge, along the darkened sidewalk, amongst the debris of construction: dirt, nails, repurposed plastic two by fours, and a row of Portable Potties.

He spent his first eight years out of high school toiling through college and an extensive graduate program until he landed a position as an associate professor of composition at the local community college. It was only temporary, he told his wife, Mel, she told her friends, and they told their children twenty-five years later. He considered himself of above average intellect— just void of real purpose and direction. "Ambition didn't always run uphill," he told his dad, who wondered why he couldn't own the community college. His friends and family referred to him, in person, as a professor even though most of his students assumed he was a volunteer. All universities made the switch to online classrooms within the pandemic-centered decade of

2020-2030. He tried a myriad of different careers on the side, but they either disagreed with his mental fortitude, finely tuned schedule of relaxation, or his educational stature. Jobs were scarce in the digital age. An industrialized man had few choices beyond tech or craftmanship, and Tapscott was handy with neither saw nor circuit board. He didn't have enough energy to take part in a pyramid scheme—top or bottom. He moved up, but the educational field was no match for pure, uncut apathy. Eventually, he became the head of the Virtual English department at Parish Community College, which gave him the raise he needed to buy a leather chair and get leather patches sewn into the elbows of two of his nine brown jackets before being hounded into retirement in his early seventies. He tried his hand at writing every decade or so but wound up drinking, arguing, sleeping, and dreadfully underpaid which made him as much a professional writer as any words on a page.

Tapscott looked in the rearview mirror, the wrinkles around Sikander's eyes reflecting back. His cocoa rich skin was dark and smooth but possessed some waves of age around his eyes. Tapscott now guessed Sikander was only ten years his junior. He saw his reflection in the mirror as well—a stark collage of blotched whites, soft, rash-like pinks, and a muted green from the ever-increasing tributary of a vein growing with every word of the conversation, matriculating from behind his left ear up to his temple, peeking from depleted groves of chalk-white hair.

"Oh, just a professor? I thought about becoming a professor once, but I make more just driving, and I didn't want to take the weekend certification class. That's why I'm still here. I wouldn't say I'm a rich, but I do make a living and work when I want. Yep, making my hours has its benefits, let me tell ya."

Tapscott's body curdled; the vein stretched across his temple.

"You know a bunch of people making money in the A/C like this?" Sikander shook his head, his bottom lip sticking out. "No, sir! Man, this is the life." Sikander's shoulders danced in the rearview as he nuzzled into the khaki seats, letting the cooling air ripple through the seats and up onto his bare, hairless calves.

Tapscott sought a path to disagree. He once would have questioned Sikander's driving. Wondered why he felt nothing was the life. Asked whether he wanted to make a mark somewhere before the dust settled and a sweaty imprint on a faux leather, futile driver's seat was all that was left of Sikander.

Where did my life turn? The thought rummaged in his innards, somewhere deep, where his hope in humanity dwindled years before. Somewhere near his thumping, heavy liver.

"Let me tell you about the time I picked up three girls from a bar—"

"No!" Tapscott said, his eyes opened, born back into the world and his puddy-colored surroundings. "I have listened past my ears' content. You, as a gainfully employed, hourly-waged chauffeur to the masses, should know how to read the cabin of your office space! I am late for an appointment. I want to get from point A to point B without the jib jab!"

"So, you—" Sikander recoiled in his seat. A blank expression of embarrassed silence materialized across his eyes.

"Without the jib and the jab!" Tapscott repeated.

Silence invaded the car's cabin like hipsters on an apple farm.

"Play the JibJab video your grandson made. Confirm?" rang into his ears, reverberating to his very core. His hands gripped the seats at his sides and his eyes tightened. Alton let out a moan for approximately nine seconds—his longest in weeks. His hand stumbled for a grip to steady himself as the car bumped over the cracks of the asphalt-covered oak roots.

CHAPTER 2

The sun crept out over the Mississippi River banks the following morning to a symphony of father figures shoving lawn mower engines as Alton and Archie Tapscott rode under twinkling shade of sagging moss-covered oak branches.

"Dad ..." Archie said as the car turned, clipping a curb. He sat cocked in the driver seat, one hand on his phone, the other holding his head up with the elbow propped against the window. "Dad?" He tried again, this time waving a soft, hairy hand—his thick, brown eyebrows strained with a yawn.

Tapscott was staring at the numerous cracks in his son's windshield.

"What are you thinking about, Dad? Talk to me, man."

"This is gonna get worse unless you fix it." He strained for-ward, scratching the windshield with a faded peach index finger. "I don't know anything about windshields, but I know that's not good."

"I've got a guy in New Orleans taking a look at it."

Alton ignored him. "I don't know if Mack will like this area of town. He doesn't know it like our neighborhood."

"This is your neighborhood. Your house is two minutes from here. I think he'll figure it out," Archie said. "Or he won't! And if he doesn't, you won't have to take care of a cat anymore. It's a win-win, really."

"How can you say that, Archie? With you down there, and your sister in Houston, Mack is almost all I've got."

Archie stared at his phone. His brown hair was combed back at all angles, long strands plunging to the back of his neck and around a vivid green polo shirt collar. His short, slim build allowed him to tuck a leg under himself while driving. A flexibility Alton had always admired.

"Oh, I know what you're thinking," Alton jumped in. "A German shepherd or a golden retriever or some expensive mixture of the two, you'd be okay with that, but a cat? It's a stigma men my age go through, I guess."

Archie glanced up for a moment. "The cat is fine ... I mean, the cat will be fine, Dad. We're right in between the house and your old office, and he knew his way up there just fine. The college is five minutes away."

"Five minutes by car. Do I need to explain the difference between a car and a cat, Archie? Don't even get me started on the havoc these hot asphalt streets will wreck on his pads. Besides," he said, settling back into his seat, "he's an entirely inside animal at this point. Domesticated after all these years. The beast you once knew, Archer, has been tamed."

"Is that why the house smelled like cat piss?"

"No, no. I cooked cauliflower last month, it lingers."

"A generation of men raised by women," Archie said with his index finger in the air like he was reciting lines.

"What in the world does that mean?" Alton asked.

"It's from Fight Club, dad. Stop cooking cauliflower."

Alton paused, sensing an argument. It was like his kids to infer rules from one-time behaviors. He'd overheard Archie telling Evelyn that their dad was a "shut-in" because he'd refused an afternoon of tee-ball crowds. Ever since Evelyn's only check-ins were to see if he was getting any sun. It's all he could get, unfortunately.

*****

Inside of the white brick guard house at the condo community's iron gate, a haphazard array of photos and papers fluttered against the walls, fighting against the draft of a blaring window unit. A frayed map of the facility's halls sat on a small desk whose tabletop was sticky with instant coffee. The smell of hard-boiled eggs permeated the paint, and Mr. E.B. Falgoust sat still in a metal swivel chair, surveying the row of eight security camera monitors, flickering in and out of their colored display. His small eyes focused on a monitor showing a herd of nuns swarming the Stations of the Cross monuments in the natural walking path area. He picked up and glanced over a digital copy of *Security Details Monthly* until a large, white SUV pulling itself up to the iron gate. He jolted to life, stiffened his back, and flattened a typed, yellow sheet over a clipboard, scanning names for those he might not be able to pronounce and looking for times. He pulled out a ruler to match the name, date, and time columns on his list and saw Alton B. Tapscott circled with red ink.

*****

"The security gate looks flimsy enough! Any cat worth half his salt might climb right over, Archie. This simply won't do. If Mack gets loose—"

"I doubt your cat can climb iron. And didn't you get him declawed?

"My God, son. Get your head out of your proverbial—"

"I mean, seriously, Dad. We're just going to look, and if you hate it, you hate it. But enough about your cat. You're more important than a cat."

"Let's just agree that whatever I think about it, there won't be any arguing."

"Sure. Whatever. At the end of the day—"

"This must be Mr. Tap-scott," came a muffled voice through the car. A sliding window jammed open as a man leaned over his elbow into the sun. His neck strained forward, twisting as if uncomfortable with the height of the window. His thin, brown hair was pulled slightly left, and a wild patch of scruff grew from his chin, sticking out multiple directions. The creases on his face matched those of a wet magazine, and his uniform appeared to be a Boy Scout's complimented with a neon orange crossing guard vest. His name badge reflected light off the sun right into the Tapscotts' eyes.

"What did he say?" Archie said.

"I don't know." Alton looked puzzled. "What did you say, sir?"

The voice grew as the neck twisted further. "I said, 'This must be Mr. Tapscott!'"

"Mr. Tapscott?" Alton questioned as he raised his thumb and index finger to the top of his nose. "What is he, five minutes my junior? He looks older than me! Why is everyone questioning my age today?"

"Dad—"

"What type of person do you have me entangled with here, son?"

"Dad—"

"You think you're confining me to this concrete abyss guarded by this—"

"*Dad!*"

"What is it?"

"Calm down. He's looking right at us."

"Well, all the more reason not to shout at your father."

Archie rolled the window down, and E.B. Falgoust proceeded with his protocol. "Well, there we are. This must be Mr. Tapscott," he said.

Groaning, Mr. Tapscott pinched the top of his nose as if popping the mother of all pimples.

"It sure is," Archie replied. "We're happy to be here."

"We?" muttered Alton.

"Well, I'm Mr. E.B. Falgoust, the security and maintenance around these grounds. I see you're here for a tour with Mr.

Murray? Oh, you'll be in good hands with Mr. Murray. Just las'
week, Mr. Murray came by the booth, and, well, hey, that's what
I call my office here …" He patted the brick frame around the
window.

Tapscott let out a groan.

"So, anyway, he comes by, and, well, you see this picture here?
This is my son, Anthony. Anthony has a son named Martin. Little
Marty is what we call him. Well, Little Marty …"

Alton's gaze drifted to a couple of planes floating in opposite
directions, their jet streams left behind like little farts. He
questioned when the last time he flew might've been, then
realized it was to Shreveport for a funeral. A thirty-five-minute
flight for a funeral.

Which friend's funeral? he wondered.

The sun was magnified through his window, pressing his
cheeks into a bright red glow. He fiddled with the air vent, hoping
the sun and not his blood pressure medicine was causing this
flash. The man at the gate was still talking,

"Well, I could probably write a book with all the things to
know about the St. Ignatius Condo Community, but …" E.B.
gazed up with a smile, pondering all there was to know.

"How about the basics?" Archie said.

E.B. continued, gathering breath.

Alton stared through the cracks in the window, through the
iron-railed gate, into the St. Ignatius Condo Community that
he feared would break his will to go out peacefully if he had any
more cheerfulness like the sort from this E.B. fellow.

Archie nodded as E.B. continued.

"You can find me here or in my condominium Mr. Murray
rents out to me and Carla in the back. See, I have this exact system,
The NannyCam 2034 System, at home and all the monitors, too."

He laughed, patting a camera. "Well, I bet you thought this old man didn't know how to set up a system that advanced? Trying to test me?" He smiled at Archie with a row of teeth, coffee and mustard entrenched between each tooth.

"No, sir, I wasn't testing you," Archie said. "I was just wondering. Let's get my dad in the gate to look around."

"Well, if it was your intention to test me, just know I have all the monitors I have here. In or out, up or over, I'm watching the gates. And recording!"

"No, I promise, Mr. E.B."

"Well, in that case, you're going to follow the driveway up to the front of the property. I'll radio ahead so they know you're coming. Give Mr. Murray my regards! Tell him E.B. sent you, he'll understand!"

"Mr. Tap-scott is on his way in," he yelled into a black hand-held radio he pulled from below. "His son is a real pistol, but you'll like him," he winked at Archie. "Say, Tap- scott, what a name. Hard as heck to pronounce. Don't hear that much down here. Scottish?"

"That'll be enough, E.B.," came a voice on the other end.

The gate slid open like a stupefied locomotive, its jangling chains grating iron dragging across the track. Start. Stop. Jerk forward. Screech a foot back. Stop again. A thought occurred to Alton.

"Excuse me, sir. What about cats?"

"Cats? Like the Broadway show?" E.B. said with a contorted face as if he stifled a giggle.

"No. I cannot express to you how serious I am—"

"Dad. Not now. We're going in."

"About the well-being and guardianship of my—"

"You're actually doing this now?"

"Cat. Mack."

"We're going, Mr. E.B.," Archie said, the car in motion, crackling down the driveway, popping acorns as it rolled through the gate.

*****

"Archie! I can't imagine why my well-being would put you in such a sour mood!" Alton reeled in his seat to face his son. "You know Mack's welfare and mine are intertwined. If anything, I should think you'd be most interested in his supervision!"

Archie's attention diverted down. "This is a work email—gimme a minute or two."

"Why did he tell us to follow the driveway? Isn't that what every driveway since the beginning of driveways was invented for? It's not like there are streetlights on driveways. That gave me a headache. That inconsolable little sycophant."

Archie sighed. "I honestly don't know, Dad. I just met him. He seems like a rube."

"Just met him? Well, you're right enough friends. "When you meet a fellow like that, especially one that works alone, you have to get in and get out. No chatting. Chatting is what your mother would have done. For hours. E.B. Falgoust would've been over for supper if she were still alive."

The car wound past rows of oak trees and azalea bushes straddling the crooked driveway. Alton regaled Archie with his recent allergy diagnosis as the car stopped in front of the St. Ignatius Condo Community's front office at a spot marked "Future Residents Only" that Alton found unamusing. "It drives itself!" Archie smirked.

A great putty-colored, stucco structure with green shutters surrounding the four glass windows, its roof rising twenty-eight feet in the air at its highest peak before cascading down toward the earth at a forty-five-degree angle on either side, sat at the end of the roundabout. The doors to the outside were white and French, as were most in south Louisiana, and one swung open hard enough to slam into a holly bush lining the sidewalk. A young woman in a bright purple dress came into view, striding toward the car. She carried a broad, eager smile and an even bigger welcome pamphlet that gave Mr. Alton Tapscott a massive headache. He'd make sure Archie noticed this one.

The balding tennis balls on his walker squished into the sidewalk, and he threw his weight onto the brown leather sandals, rising with a creak. He got out of the car, slamming the door so the window rattled. The sound of old joints and rattling chains rang from a distance as the iron gate crept to a violent close.

"Well, this must be, Mr. Tapscott." She slid on the side of the walker and gave familiar hug, squeezing his shoulders with one arm. "Welcome to St. Ignatius! Usually, the nuns are here to greet new tenants, but you came early, and they're all probably praying or something." She introduced herself as Samantha Cleary, the front desk clerk and activities director.

He raised a suspecting eyebrow in Archie's direction. This was the best this place could do? He began to reason in his head. *So, replace a few nuns with a young harlot and expect me to sign on a dotted line, eh? I've been getting a haircut at a sports bar salon hybrid for years and it recently transitioned into full on gentlemen's club—with haircuts—so I know about harlots, and they would have to do better than this.*

"That's no problem," Archie said. "Dad's just excited to see the place." There was warmth in Archie's tone as he let go of the walker and shuffled forward.

She strode through the front, opening the second swinging French door to let Alton squeeze in, stopping only for a moment inside of the front lobby to sign the visitor's log. A table in the corner was piled high with pinatas, another with red wrapping paper. The ceilings were tall and lofted, a faint blue wood, and four small lamps glowed from four small wooden tables in the corners, just enough to make the room visible without showing scuffs in the paint. The floors appeared old and wooden, and Alton liked what he thought was the secure footing of a concrete foundation. The solid wood changed to white tile as they entered the hallway, scanning a show room. Its bed was pristinely made, and its kitchen's counters reflected the color of your eyes. All the plastic vases overflowed with plastic flowers. Ms. Cleary assured them each room was LIZA compatible.

He saw his reflection in the floor well enough to notice a line of sweat smearing across the underside of his pant exterior. The clanking of metal and feet mixed with the clamor of voices stirred toward the clubhouse as Ms. Cleary rounded the corner with the Tapscott men in tow.

"We're almost there," she said.

"Well, you still haven't even begun to answer my question, young lady. Does St. Ignatius offer rides to the vet? This is a matter of most importance, you see."

Archie grabbed his dad's shoulder. "Dad, we get it ... you are concerned. Sam has already mentioned she doesn't know the answer, but that she'll find out soon. Take a deep breath, why don't you?"

"Oh, everything is fine!" Tapscott threw up his hands and waved them like the good Lord intended, his face a wild grouse. "Why would anyone worry? I'm just here, wondering if the only companion I've had for the last nine years," he looked at Archie, "will be near me at the end of it all!"

Archie removed his hand from his dad's shoulder, allowing

Tapscott the flexibility to pound his Simpson's medical-grade, deluxe, two-button, folding, aluminum walker onto the Spanish-tile of the hallway with each word of his next outburst. "I. Need. To. Go. To. The. Bathroom!"

"Gentlemen!" a voice called around the corner. "Please, come on in."

Archie released an elongated sigh, and the trio entered the expanse of the green clubhouse room.

*****

Mr. Cooper Murray was a tall man. His shirts consisted of pastels across the spectrum, linens as thin as a blade of Bermuda, and wind suits that would break even the warmest of summer breezes. Murray's copper hair, deliberately sprayed and brushed to one side, made you believe he emerged from the womb with that hairstyle. It never moved. A pair of gold, horn-rimmed glasses perched near the tip of his nose.

The day he met Tapscott in the green carpeted, wood-paneled clubhouse of St. Ignatius, Mr. Murray was wearing a pair of white saddle shoes that somehow matched his peach, short-sleeve button down. His belt was stitched with tiny yacht flags against a blue sky.

Murray was waiting for his guests to arrive while he properly positioned his elbow on the mantle of the den's fireplace which he lowered four years prior for this exact reason. Tapscott needed to use the bathroom. Nonetheless, he was still here, his corduroy pants blending in with the beige couch sitting atop the worn, green carpet.

Tapscott watched the brightly dressed chap prattling on about the community's history, only breaking script when he corrected Archie on the preferred terminology for St. Ignatius—

an assisted living or retirement community, not a nursing home. Retirement, not rehab, he repeated. This gave the impression that all the residents chewed bananas without assistance. Tapscott found the peach-shirted man to be exactly as the ghastly fellow at the gate described—someone with which he did not want to associate.

Murray grabbed Alton's hand and elbow when they'd come into the room, as if he'd shake his head but steady Alton at the same time. "Oh, nice grip," Murray said. "You can tell a lot about a man from a good grip, and you've got one." He was yelling.

Archie peppered the man with questions about the lifestyle of an Ignatius resident as Mr. Murray passed out pamphlets. Each had a couple sitting with bright dentures smiling from a bench as they waved to a man on a walking path whose expiration date looked closer than he might expect. The grass appeared to be freshly cut, and, judging by their smiles, the couple freshly married. The husband looked to be four to five years older than the wife, whose hair took the color and shape of a new volleyball.

Murry was talking as Tapscott snuck off to the bathroom, and when he returned, Murry was still talking.

"And here is our information on sexual intercourse with the elderly—"

A pamphlet on the table caught Tapscott's eye. It displayed the usual past-their-prime couple, but this time the old man was walking with a dog.

"Excuse me!" he interrupted the conversation. "I noticed the walking-path model in this particular pamphlet is shown with a canine … a dog."

Murray began to nod and shot a confused glance Archie's way.

"Are animals allowed on the grounds? What about in the actual apartments?"

Mr. Murray stopped nodding and looked toward Archie with his hands suspended in motion.

"Dad," Archie stood, glazing over at a painting above the mantle. "Dad," he began again, "Mr. Murray was just saying … please try to keep up. He does this, Mr. Murray."

"Oh, Archie, you can call me Cooper. I think we'll be well familiar by the time your dad moves in anyhow."

"So, is that a yes?" Tapscott hadn't stopped staring at the man with the dog. He scoured the glossy pages for a picture of an old woman sitting by a T.V. with a cat, but only saw sitting dogs and one picture of a woman with binoculars staring through her window at a blue jay. The latter image scared him to some degree. He hated blue jays as he often found them sitting in the willow above his old Subaru in the driveway, and he assumed them to be the perpetrators of what he called a Baton Rouge snowstorm … bird shit. The prospect of being in the company of such dimwitted simpletons such as this woman and her binoculars made his gastro-intestinal system bubble.

"Well, Dad, it's a yes and a no. You see, dogs are okay, but—"

"Oh God!" Mr. Tapscott shouted as he threw his body back into the couch cushions. "Don't tell me this place is going to be like that bar you absconded me off to last year! The barking! The stupidity! And their owners." He was laughing … the dogs barking at each other while people screamed over the sound of a nearby TV. "I'll tell ya, Murphy, is it? It's almost enough to make a man stop drinking."

He'd attempted to bring Mack there a month after his first visit, only to be turned away since the cat upset the dogs. After a rousing rendition of Langston Hughes' "I, Too, Sing America," he was escorted off the property.

"If this is going to be the case," Tapscott said, straightening both his posture and index finger, "I simply cannot stay. Let's go, Archie."

"Well, h-hold up, Mr. Tap-scott." Mr. Murray lurched forward from where he was leaning on the arm of a leather chair. "Let's take the tour of St. Ignatius before you make any decisions. Besides, these aren't actual dogs in these photos. These are Joy for All Robotic Companions for Seniors. But it fooled you, didn't it? Let's see if we can't find one you'll like."

"Dad, take the tour. Please. I drove all the way up."

"Ahh, yes. How could I forget the hour drive you made?"

"Mr. Tap-scott, the Devil is in the details, is it not?" Murray said. "Let me take you around, show you the grounds, show you what your life would look like here at St. Ignatius. If you don't love it, then, hey, it was nice meeting the two of you anyway—don't often get to make new friends at my age. Just let me show you first." Murray's smile was comfortable, neither strained nor forced.

It reminded Tapscott of his older brother's. Not enough to buckle any women's knees but maybe just enough to convince you to do something stupid. Something about his natural teeth made him more trustable than a first instinct suggested. In a world of dentures and veneers, it was reassuring to see a person live with what God, or genetics, gave them.

"Come on, Dad. I'm sure you'll enjoy yourself."

"Actually, I was thinking that Ms. Cleary," who materialized again at the doorway, "could take you, Archie, to the dining room and chapel while your father and I explore some of the property they don't show you on the pamphlets."

Time without Archie was exactly what Alton needed to get out of this place without having to put up much of a fight, he decided. A quick tour and he'd be out of there like a dwarf in a canon … and just in time to make the early bird lunch special at Zippy's. Two frozen margaritas in the morning heat, and he'd wind up enough courage to call into a radio show or two.

"Sounds good to me! Don't wait up, Archie!" Mr. Tapscott chuckled as he rose to meet his Simpson's walker.

CHAPTER 3

Alton Tapscott studied the large printout of the St. Ignatius grounds—the chapel to the gardens, to the shitters, to the pissers in the chapel—with "YOU ARE HERE" in big, bold letters on top of the clubhouse, staring down on him. St Ignatius Retirement Community was an eight-acre property with four separate buildings and one small chapel. The clubhouse was the crown jewel and sat at the front of the property. The green rug ran throughout the room except for the dining hall, which was covered in an appropriate linoleum square tile—suitable for cleaning, especially on soup night, which happened to be every weekday.

The map positioned the other three buildings to the north, east, and west of the clubhouse, the chapel alone in the center.

"Thought your son would never let us get started," Mr. Murray said as the two of them walked outside.

"Yeah, Archie can be a little too hands-on. His mother was, too."

"My boys used to be that way. Trust me. But, once their mother left us ten years back, they just about dropped me off here before her casket even had time to get dirty."

Tapscott was surprised, but he didn't know why. "Damn shame. Archie just wants me here because his doctor buddy recommended I have a twenty-four hour nurse."

"Damn shame," Murray echoed. "But we are getting older, Alton."

"You can call me Tapscott," Tapscott always felt the name Alton to be a bit formal until he reached his sixties, but by then he wasn't used to it, "and I'm advancing in age, sure, but my weight is advancing a little more aggressively. First the nurse was for the blood pressure, then the hip, then the knees, but I've lost count of all the reasons he said I needed one by now."

"Tapscott, if I've learned anything during my time here," Murray stopped along the path, "it's that this is your new family. Archie can come visit when he pleases, but, now trust me on this, stick with me and this community will accept you. Just don't let the other tenants get you down. I think they're a bit intimidated by me. They're a sickly lot … between you and me. Trust me. But we've got a good group of walkie-talkies here. Trust me."

A walkie-talkie was a resident that could walk and talk, explained Cooper. "A lot of retirement homes don't have them like we do, but we've got a bunch. Few wheelchairs and fewer mutes. Hell, most of them speak with more sense than E.B."

Tapscott felt a sense of comfort around Cooper Murray even though he was tall and he dressed to standards Tapscott tended to avoid. He also felt some pride at ascending the social ranks by showing ability to walk and talk and often in unison. A stroll around an old folks' home, Tapscott decided, wasn't the worst way to get his physician-recommended steps in for the day, and this way he wouldn't have to climb and strap his step counter on the ceiling fan later.

After passing under a red roof tiled arched breezeway, the two turned a corner, and the brightness of the sun caused Tapscott to stop and sneeze. *Strike one. They'll take me for a plague rat*, he surmised with a smile.

The path stretched forward until it sat under the gaze of two large, square buildings with small, wooden fences around the sides and back of each. Grass sprouted from the concrete walkway, and a small fountain gurgled to life, spewing in all directions. A bench, drenched from the fountain, encircled it. Tapscott sensed each building accounted for two separate apartments, connected by what he thought was an inner wall, and the residential apartments, two by two, and side by side, edged a sprawling gray, sandy concrete courtyard—an ode to Baton Rouge's urban developments in the early 20-teens. Each apartment was connected to another, then separated by a golf-kart parking spot the size of the EZGO RXV 3.0 that came with the lease.

The raised, covered concrete porches were safe from the sun and fountain spew, and two rocking chairs, but tenants mostly sat on their own and hollered across the courtyard. The acoustics, needless to say, were outstanding.

Alton saw a row of tenants perched on porches, like a job fair in a gymnasium.

"Well, here they are. A real murders' row," Murray said. "If you feel yourself falling asleep or getting annoyed, grab my arm and we'll make a run for it."

He winked.

*****

"Mr. Alton Tapscott, let me introduce you to Ms. Poppy Burt. Ms. Burt," Murray raised his volume and leaned in toward an old woman sitting on a stoop, "this is Mr. Tapscott. He's thinking about coming to our community soon."

"I can hear just fine, Cooper," the woman said as she extended a hand that connected her fingers to a sponge of a forearm. Her biceps flapped out of her shirt sleeve like an uncooked split sausage. Her shirt was bright red with the words "Donkeys belong in a barn," with an elephant holding a gavel. A small visor sat idly atop a cauliflower head of hair.

Her porch was adorned with four different American flags, including one made into a pillow that sat on a yellow folding chair with the image of a snake stretching toward the sky.

"Alton Tapscott. Alton is my first name, Ms. Burt."

"Well, isn't that nice. Welcome to St. Ignatius. Is that Scottish? You can call me Poppy by the way."

"You an animal lover, Ms. Poppy?" he said, gesturing with his eyes over to her throw pillow.

"I love eating 'em if that's what you mean." Her skin coiled as she smiled. "But some people think they're only for petting." She glanced to the brick wall to her right and then winked, causing him to smile and nod as if it were something he understood. "You lookin' at my nail pole-ish. It's called Tiger Blood." She flashed her hand in front of her face and wriggled her fingers. "I read somewhere it was good to have bright nail pole-ish if you live in a flood zone, so at least they see you waving when it's dark out. Not that we flood here but every s'often."

Tapscott exchanged good-byes with Ms. Burt while Murray was dragging him to the next porch. "Had to get you out of there while we're still young," Murray said. "She, um, likes to talk, especially about her precious politics. She's also a terrible racist, Mr. Tapscott, but she'll be dead before the next election. An old widow."

He was relieved Murray seemed equally annoyed with her.

Ms. Burt's apartment shared a wall with Mr. Camille Renata. Originally from France, Renata explained, he came to America to work in New York City in the early 2030s. Finding the work pace and the street population overbearing, he moved to New Orleans where he found a home amongst the social elite on St. Charles Avenue. He ended up in Baton Rouge after a rather unfortunate night of drunken political festering and discussions that he didn't share with Tapscott at the time. He fled north and sought social refuge amongst the smaller parade routes of Spanish Town in Baton Rouge. He had a thin build—scrawny, malnourished in the way that gives you a small paunch belly—and his white face had small, gold, octagonal eyeglasses pressed against his eyelids.

Mr. Renata's accent sounded like equal parts French, Yankee, and Yat; slow but steady like a mouthful of grapes.

Renata's porch also had American flags, albeit fewer animals with agendas. His shirt resembled the color of those snow melt lakes Tapscott saw in Canada once, a long time ago. The Earth stared at him and Murray from the front of Renata's shirt, two eyes and a smile, with little arms and white gloves extending to the side. "Hug The Earth, Don't Drug the Soil," was in bright green lettering across the top.

There were several signs in the window behind Renata. One read "My Body, My Rules," another, "I'm With Them," another, "LGBTTQQIAAP." Alton tried to decipher the last one in his head, and Renata perked up.

"Oh, I used those years, years ago. But, strangely, some people still haven't come around to them!" He craned his neck as if he'd extend it around the corner. "Do you recognize the many forms the human life goes through on its way to the final resting place, Mr. Tapscott?"

"I, um, I don't know if I know them all?"

Letting out a laugh, Mr. Renata leaned on the brick pillar outside his door. "Well, nobody knows them all, Mr. Tapscott. That's why we live!" He patted Tapscott on the shoulder and winked as Mr. Murray bid Camille Renata adieu.

"What was that?" he asked Murray.

"If I knew … Well, if I knew, I'd probably speak to that man more often." Mr. Murray shook his head. "I just say nine o'clock is too late to discuss much of anything, but they disagree. A bona fide flake, Alton."

Tapscott nodded hard enough that his hair flopped to his forehead. According to him, nine o'clock was the new eleven o'clock. His favorite show, *Celebrity Russian Roulette*, ended at eight-thirty, and after a short hygiene routine, he was always in bed before nine, or at least asleep on the couch.

The men moved across the courtyard to the next apartment pairing. There was a crucifix hanging on one door, and a small concrete statue resembling a man in robes grew from the dirt patch in front of the porch, a saint of some sort, he assumed. The porch's occupant, Mrs. Cricket Kirby, was a pint-sized, plump woman in a kimono. Murray appeared to introduce the feebler, less-alert residents by their Christian names with a proper heading.

"Hello there, Mrs. Kirby!"

"Well, hello back, *Mister* Murray," she said through a welcoming grin. Her blonde hair, bright even in the cover of the porch, frizzed around her scalp to form a static globe. She seemed to strain with her smile, revealing a pair of emotional green eyes, light and warm. A copy of *Catholic Community Monthly* sagged on her knees.

"I like your statue, Mrs. Kirby," Tapscott murmured.

"Oh, you do? My husband can't stand it." Her pink and plush cheeks wrinkled when she smiled and spoke, her phrases spaced by heavy breaths. "It's Saint Joseph. You must be a religious man, Mr. Tapscott?" she said, her head tottering to one side, almost as if studying his piousness.

"I dabble. A eucharist here, a confession there. But it's been hard to get to church the last few decades ... especially after the last couple of pandemics."

"Oh, well you're sure right. Last one almost got my Mr. Kirby," she said, nodding.

"But we had it under control well enough," Murray interjected. "Only three deaths out of fourteen infections which was half the national rate."

"Oh, right. Sure. Well, you'll like it here, Mr. Tapscott. Mass every day at five a.m., then the stations of the cross, then again before supper at four." She leaned in closer on her rocker and whispered, "And when someone dies, we always get a rosary!"

"That'll be all, dear." Murray motioned for Alton to make an exit.

"It was nice meeting you, Mr. Tapscott. And I'll say a prayer you find peace!"

In the apartment next door, he met a man that stood to shake hands, revealing a fat stomach with a gray-collared shirt and pear-shaped legs that slanted off his rocker, feet waving inches from the floor when he sat back down. He resembled his wife's canonized concrete yard ornament, his pants pulled near his abdomen after misplacing his waistline. Cliff was a deacon at Our Lady of Mercy just down the street until he retired to the home a few years prior, he told Alton.

The Kirby patriarch smiled and nodded as Murray explained Tapscott's current circumstance. Smiled and nodded when he heard about Alton's kids living out of town. Smiled and nodded when they departed. Smiled and nodded when his wife crept over to ask what he thought about Tapscott. Grimaced when he tried to sit back down in his lawn chair.

"That's a beaten man, Alton," Murray said, feet from Mr. Kirby. "That wife of his would kill you or me. It's a miracle he's made it this long."

"Almost makes you believe in a higher power." Alton watched cautiously for Murray's reaction. Murray missed this last remark, and Alton was relieved. He didn't mean it. "And you can call me Tapscott."

He'd attended Sunday school ever since his mother found it much easier to kneel, stand, sit, and reconcile with her feelings for the pool boy without a sweating, squirming blob of linen in her arms. He graduated to drawing cartoons on the pages of the hymnal and sleeping under the pews. He was always dressed in his best ill-fitting slacks and shirt, unlike the Engelbert sisters, Mary Lee and Mary Ann, who got to wear Umbro shorts and T-shirts. If you're going to draw on Luke's Gospel, you might as well be in khaki pants, his mom would say.

Tapscott's mother had a propensity to pray out loud. Once, while he was in the midst of changing Daniel's fate in the lion's den with a number 2 pencil, his mother lurched forward to grab her rosary.

"For Pope Benedict," she started. His pencil continued to sketch a roaring lion's mane. "For the unfortunate," as the lead traced a bone protruding from a gnarled arm. "For the poor," she whispered. A gray pool of blood was beginning to form just above the second reading, Daniel's fate was all but sealed.

"And, please, for my Alton. We've spoken about him, but he can't find your grace." Daniel lived to see another century. He had a reservation in his mother's prayer in perpetuity, especially after she caught him masturbating to a photo of the family on a fishing trip. An unfortunate product of the panel sliding digital photo frame in the family's guest bathroom. It wasn't as bad as it looked, he'd pleaded.

"It was a picture of Aunt Sharon before that one, I swear to God!"

*****

Mr. Zach Majoria was a veteran of the Iraq war according to the white oval "IRQ" sticker on the apartment window. He had a slim build and his T-shirt draped him like a clothesline. He talked about his immigration to the U.S. via adoption in 1999, and they discussed a shared love of the History Channel. The flat front of his olive face hung under a mop of grizzly-colored hair.

"Thanks for your service... I guess..." Tapscott said, not knowing the correct greeting for a war so lost to history. Mr. Majoria shrugged.

Mr. Nick Romero was next door. Romero was an I.T. tech for a start-up in the 2000s, and he remained with the company until it closed the month before his pension. He sat in a petulant position, arms crossed and barely looking up to shake Tapscott's hand. When he did, it was a dry, lifeless hand that felt like a Latex glove.

Murray filled him in that the pair dated for a brief period when Romero first moved in. There was an unceremonious breaking of the couple a few short months later. They were getting on in age and getting it on each night, sometimes after nine o'clock. This caused a small kerfuffle over who got their limited supply of government issued erectile dysfunction contraband each night. Romero told E.B. the fight was over the cheese on a pizza.

"Well, now, Mr. Romero told me Mr. Majoria, you see, he likes to put the cheese on the pizza. Mr. Romero wanted Mr. Majoria to let me, Mr. Romero, put the cheese on the pizza every now and then. Not every night, you hear? Just a couple of nights a week. Something about Mr. Majoria always got to eat the cheese and it was hard for Mr. Romero to enjoy his pizza without some cheese, too. Couple of bozos is what Mr. Murray will tell ya." E.B. told this story to each nurse before they checked Romero's or Majoria's cholesterol, fearing unusually high mozzarella numbers.

"You'll want to steer clear of those two," Murray said. "Some people just don't take life as seriously as they should, Tap. Did you see the state of Nick's damn shirt? You try to put together a decent tour, but these bozos can't keep it together for fifteen minutes. I'll tell you, Scott ... er, Tapscott, they don't make 'em like us anymore."

Next, he met the Rudolphs—Donald and Jessie. They were the only black couple in the community, Murray made a point of saying, and shared an apartment, unlike the Kirbys. After fifty-seven years, Mr. Rudolph hadn't quite driven Jessie to the other side of a drywall. They were pleasant enough.

"They mainly keep to themselves, which makes me wonder. A little too lovey-dovey for me, too," Murray said.

"I was thinking the same. It's not natural to be that close to another person."

Tapscott met more senior citizens than a Ft. Lauderdale mayoral candidate. The Warners, the Kershaws, and the Prudhomes met every evening for tea. Murray was tired of their routine. The Wybles played Mahjong with the Rows, but the

Heberts thought that was a bit too foreign for their tastes, but the Rows invited him anyway. The Heberts preferred Texas Hold 'Em on Tuesday nights. Murray couldn't stand gambling. Tapscott agreed it probably wasn't socially acceptable at their age though he enjoyed his one visit to Las Vegas decades before—despite Spiderman and Elvis going for his wallet late one night.

North of the clubhouse and northwest of the tenant apartments, they saw the fitness center and courts. The fitness center consisted of a sauna and steam room, majoring on the conceptualization and interpretation of the ever-evolving human form and minoring in the art of speaking to someone without looking below their neckline.

Tennis, shuffleboard, chess, and croquet made up the St. Ignatius court system. The tennis court was the only grass structure of its kind within four hundred miles, which was exciting to the two tennis enthusiasts on-site and their physical therapists.

Northwest of the clubhouse, due west of the apartments, and southwest of the courts sat the library, theater, and convent. The library was an extensive record of DVDs, computers, and encyclopedia collections missing between one and several letters in the anthology. Tapscott scanned the shelves looking for the Louisiana State University journal publication of his short story from his undergraduate years, but the library didn't carry it. It must've been lost, he hoped, in a recent flood. The bottom three rows of each shelf were empty, their foundations still lined with a waving mold mosaic marking the top of the water line.

The theater on the grounds, which Murray insisted should be spelled "Theatre" on the map, was home to several adapted dramas and one-woman shows performed by the previous facility owner's aging daughter. She was living off money her father made in the sale of St. Ignatius, but she was living on the applause from the cracked-skin crowd of four to five residents that made their way in to see her fifth performance of the befuddling "The Landlord's Daughter" about a young mistress realizing her true calling was, in fact, nothing. She was born to play the role.

The convent served the nuns that roamed the St. Ignatius campus. Tapscott met several in procession from mass, all black robes and white Ked sneakers squishing across the pavement. It was more of a spiritual retirement home in itself, he thought. God was alive and well in south Louisiana, but more recently, after President Dwayne Johnson decreed the minimum wage too low at $33.50 an hour, vows of poverty took a proverbial hit. With a dwindling talent pool, the nuns in the area became old and gray, God willing, and the empty rooms in the convent were now storage for even more DVDs, computers, and previously lost encyclopedia collections—and Apple products. This generation liked to call themselves minimalists, but that's because all their belongings fit in a hard drive.

"Well, Tap," Murray surveyed the St. Ignatius campus from the chapel steps just before dusk, "whatcha think?"

He let the question slosh around his head while he looked for a graceful exit, and he grew thankful, as he pondered moving into a home with the expectation of dying, that he'd soon be back on the couch at his home. His back straightened and he gripped his walker's handles, nodding to each corner of the grounds.

"This was certainly an interesting day, Murray," he said. "Never thought I'd move out of Mel and I's house. Our house is home, but this gives me something to think about, for sure. Nice place you have here. Nice place. Just maybe not for me, at this time, you understand, Cooper? I am sorry to say your Pet Policy is a deal-breaker." He'd endured the day well enough. Missed a few episodes and major plot points of some staple television programs, but he'd be back in his chair with Mack on his lap soon. He'd gone on the tour, had met Archie halfway on this one. Before finding the next tour, he'd make Archie go through some more hoops ... maybe one with a view of the river. He smirked.

"Well, I'm glad to at least hear you liked it," Murray said. "I think you're going to like it here."

"Except for your pet rules, Cooper, it was a good tour. And maybe someday we can get together for a margarita or something."

"This is what's best," Murray said, putting his arm around Alton and turning him around until the entire campus came into view.

The sunset danced on the windows of the chapel. The blood orange sun melted into the horizon and snuck through the thick oak branches to illuminate the eight acres of St. Ignatius Condo Community. Because this region produced more oil and natural gas in the later part of the 20th century than almost anywhere in the world, the fumes from the nearby plants mixed with other strange gasses in the sky to produce a Mars skyline, as if a refinery blowout stretched across the entire horizon. At any rate, it was beautiful.

Tapscott drank it in before a sound like a screech owl broke his concentration. A large figure in what appeared to be a Velcro brazier was hoisting a piece of furniture while a rickety, squeaking dolly labored underneath, screaming out. Tapscott saw as E.B. helped the man maneuver the chair through a small doorway, disappearing into a dark apartment.

The chair had been a muted hunter green with small, brown monkeys embroidered here and there. There were stains on the back where kids spilled juice, or a dog satisfied a back itch for too long. Scratches, rips, and tears down the left armrest could only belong to a cat or an indoor weed eater. The chair had been sat on, slept in, and endured a slight uptick in urine exposure in recent years.

Alton Tapscott looked up at Cooper Murray. "What the fuck is my chair doing here?"

*****

Tapscott shut the door to his new apartment at almost nine o'clock. He'd yet to eat or scratch his ass since they told him Archie left halfway through the tour. Surrounded by people he didn't know on the linoleum-lined St. Ignatius lobby, Tapscott went to fighting like a cat out of water. His walker turned into a perfect shield to fend off multiple black men in matching green uniforms.

"Stay back, ingrates! Return my belongings and I'll go without a fuss!"

A young orderly on his second day of training stepped forward and met the brunt end of a grizzled tennis ball.

"Where is Archie, LIZA?" His heart rate was up and his head in a tailspin. His mind dug into one name, encircling Archie in brain like a starved flock. "Call Archie, LIZA! Confirm."

"Tapscott, this is what Archie wanted," Murray muttered from behind the small, green phalanx of orderlies.

"Not now, Murray. I need to go home!"

"*Call canceled.*"

"No, LIZA. Call Archie!"

"*Mr. Archie is currently in do not disturb mode. Is there anything else I can help you with?*"

He lowered his walker and leaned on the handles, sucking air through his nose and mouth as the orderlies swarmed him, attempting to both hold him up and restrain him.

"This is what's best," Murray said as his hand landed on Tapscott's shoulder. "You can start living your life again. You're part of the St. Ignatius family now. This is what's best. We'll bend the pet policy if that's what it takes."

*****

Tapscott turned to survey his room. The green chair sat in a corner facing a small TV centered on the opposite wall. The rug was a Navajo print Pendleton he'd bought while in Colorado in 2024. It made him seem like more of an American outdoorsman while being comfortable enough to keep him locked inside. A small, brass lamp was in the corner, its shade a faded yellow with flying duck silhouettes outlined on around the middle. The lamp was a gift from his father, an actual American outdoorsman, and served as a good reminder that brass used to be a trend in home decor. A tremendous yellow love seat was across from the chair and lamp. His old bookcase sat below the mounted TV with a mob of papers and binders and utensils spilling over the edge of each shelf, thrown into their place by the moving men. He saw no cat.

Past the living room sat a small, circular dining table and two chairs. The table had glistening white wooden legs and a laminated turquoise top. It came with four chairs with turquoise cushions when his grandmother picked it up from a consignment store back in the 1950s. The seat's pillows emitted a slow whoosh when anyone, large or small, took a seat. It embarrassed his daughter when she brought her husband home to meet the family, but the chairs were a gentle reminder that turquoise was once a trend in home decor, so Tapscott never got them refinished. The other two turquoise chairs were M.I.A.

The spartan kitchen included a white refrigerator with different life insurance salesmen magnets at the top, a microwave with three settings: popcorn, soup, and hot dog. The LIZA-compatible stove sat near a small window with a view of the grounds' interior brick wall five feet away. Archie always wanted his dad to get LIZA-compatible appliances, so he wouldn't overcook food, or forget to turn off the stove, or let the gas run for thirty minutes and light a match ... ending it all on his terms. The basics. The fluorescent light above flickered.

There was no sign of Mack at all. They lied to him, he now guessed.

A minuscule bathroom sat in between the kitchen and his new bedroom. His old, white shower curtain dangled from the rings above his handicap-accessible shower-bath combination. The sight of two sinks made him smile for a brief moment in time. His wife always wanted a master bath with two sinks.

His dresser sat against the far wall of the bedroom, halfway covering the front window, and his bed was already draped by his old guest room comforter from his house. The pictures on the wall were mainly old baseball stadiums that he'd taken Archie to—gifts he'd given to Archie after a salesman suckered his dad into buying a stadium photography subscription. Kellogg's Tony the Tiger Stadium in Detroit to see a band Archie loved, GoldBond Foot Powder Arena to see Archie's favorite basketball team, and the Disney Dome, where he took Archie to see a man juggle chainsaws, hung above the headboard. The blinds were thick and white.

He sat down, looked around, and remembered where he'd been this morning; making eggs on his stove, in his house, on his street. The wood floors creaking with every step. The pier and beam foundation, at first an affordable option to younger couples on a shoestring budget, were now a reliable defense against flooding. The crown molding stretched across the entire ceiling, and the archway from the living room to the hallway were a real showstopper with the realtor back when Tapscott bought the house. The swinging door from the kitchen separated whatever odor emitted from the stove since the hood vent fan broke decades before. And the walls of his cottage—Seattle Gray—painted the first month after they bought the house. He remembered it came out bluer than gray, but they couldn't afford more.

The feeling started in his gut and meandered to his chest and throat. The new apartment closed in around him. He noticed the walls were a dingy, pale khaki color. A soft numbness took hold of his fingers and brain as his upper half fell back into the bed, and he thought he was having a heart attack. He hoped he was having a heart attack as he realized he was, quite possibly for the first time since he was born, completely alone—in a room crowded with his belongings yet bare and sparse in resemblance to home.

He'd spent years by himself, not a human soul around, in his home, with his pictures, his old banister that needed fixing, his toilet seat, and his poorly tended backyard. A baseball from his high school days, some CDs and DVDs from his exhaustive streaming-service boycott days. "The things you own end up owning you," Archie said on a visit last month. Another movie quote, Alton's LIZA confirmed. Now he was like a freshman in a boarding school dorm, except most first-year students in boarding school dorm rooms make it out alive ... or so he imagined. The idea crawled across his skin and made him shake. He tried to lift his head, but it was too heavy.

He asked LIZA of Mack's whereabouts, but she didn't locate his collar. He must be at least a hundred yards away, or else she'd find him. Tapscott imagined one of the stray dogs getting to Mack, or some dipshit from the pound scooping him up, or another dipshit with an air rifle shooting what they thought to be a feral cat. Too many dipshits out there these days.

He tried to work the TV, but it didn't have his channels. Ordinarily, he'd call Archie to get his input on the best show to watch, how streaming works now, or how to connect LIZA to the TV, but he must be on the run now, flying down I-10. He remembered holding Archie for the first time in the delivery room. The birth took forty-five seconds in total—one push. He just slid out, almost right into Tapscott's arms, and he held Archie's hands before pinching his knees and toes, both smiling and crying.

The kitchen light flickered, and the fridge's ice machine kicked up, creating a loud humming from the kitchen. He tried sitting up and inched his way to the green monkey chair.

"LIZA, find Mack."

"*Cannot locate at this time.*"

"LIZA, find Mack."

"*Cannot locate at this time.*"

He just about spit his milk all nine feet across the room when the cat sprung on the armrest next to him, his orange fur damp and musty. He exclaimed relief and checked the cat for anything out of the ordinary—his collar was either broken or LIZA was.

"How did you get here?"

Did Archie put him in his crate? Tapscott wondered. *And when?*

"He knows you hate that damn thing," he muttered through a soft film of tears, rubbing the cat's neck.

"Did they bring food? Doesn't matter," he assured Mack. They'd share if necessary.

Mack sniffed then sampled a cold, small cup of cream corn from the welcome basket next to the monthly newsletter, activity schedule, and a forty-ounce bottle of prune juice with a blue bow on top. "*The South's Best Creamed Corn!*" was written on the lid in red script. The pale hill jiggled in the bowl, reflecting the haze from the lamp.

Tapscott turned the lamp off, closed his eyes, and licked the bowl clean. LIZA turned on the TV, and Mack nuzzled into the rolls of flannel and corduroy as the two Tapscott men dozed off under the fuzzy glow of *Extreme Cupcake Baking Deathmatch*: *Season Two*.

CHAPTER 4

Alton Tapscott met the nurses his first morning, the housekeeping staff the second. He brainstormed ways out of the condo community. Unless he could scale a wall, cat and chair in tow, it was hopeless. He took his meals in his apartment and tried dialing Archie each morning but without success. The complimentary bulky, wooden shades in the living room blocked out enough light that the room and floors stayed cool, even in the afternoon heat. He saw the neighbors sat outside in the mornings, then retreated around noon when the heat and humidity beat on, but they made little attempt at luring him out of the house. His duplex mate was M.I.A., but Tapscott heard through the drywall that the man fell asleep to the sounds of the eighty-third season of *The Bachelor*, so he was a man of taste.

*****

Like a teenager after a video game binge, he sluffed across the wooden floor and the frigid bathroom tile on day three. A slow dribble splattered across the seat, his aim settling in like a trained Jedi.

"Oh, okay. Ooookayyy … here we go." His eyes fighting hard to stay open, he progressed. Then a loud bang came from the from the front door.

"Shit!" Tapscott winced, urine splattering the seat, walls, and walker.

The knocking continued enough for a small, framed painting of a sailboat to sway on its nail.

"Tapscott! You up?" came a voice muffled from outside. "Time to get going!"

"I'm here!" Tapscott shouted, almost to himself. Wetting the corners of his lips, he smacked the dried ridges of his mouth open and felt the crackling skin open. "I'm up!" He fumbled with his robe, using the ultra-thin toilet paper to clean the tops of his feet.

The buzzing window unit dripped on the apartment floor and made the bathroom mirror sweat. Keys jingled outside of his door, and his pace quickened. The door swung open, and Cooper Murray stood in the frame in khaki pants made entirely of starch, an embroidered belt with golf balls and clubs and a pastel purple shirt, initials CM on the left breast pocket.

"Cooper!" Tapscott shouted, whipping away some excess dribble on his underwear.

"Tap-scott! Good morning. I didn't wake you up, did I?"

"N-No. I'd been up for a little bit," he said as he squinted through the morning glare streaming through the door. He noted Murray's hair was combed, and he began brushing his unkempt mop of sandy brown hair over the pale streaks of skin shining through as if carved from an icecream scooper. He was attempting to tie his robe's waist belt with such concentration that he didn't notice E.B. Falgoust lurking in the doorway behind Murray.

"Okay, Tapscott. Let's get going," E.B. shouted, scaring Tapscott enough to let out a little more wetness on his cloth boxers.

"Going? I'm in my—"

"It's almost 6:45. We've got bingo."

Tapscott would soon find that on a day like today—a Tuesday, or Wednesday, or any other day than Sunday—the ancient art of bingo ruled the roost. This was an easy way for dementia and Alzheimer residents to flex their short-term memory muscles, and for the rest of the campus, bingo was an opportunity for a quick buck.

"I appreciate you checking on me, but at this hour, and after the days I've had ..." He paused, letting the thought drift.

"Oh, nonsense, Scott. Let's get you out of this damp place." Murray checked the thermostat, and without hesitation, clicked the thermostat pad up a few degrees. "We'll stop and get you some breakfast along the way. Oh, here he is!"

Murray bent down and inspected the orange ball of fur nuzzled into the corner of the green monkey chair. "Someone got lucky to be here, didn't he?"

"I'm not even wearing clothes and haven't had a proper breakfast. I'll see you another time," Tapscott said, still struggling to get both ends of the robe's belt in each hand.

"No, no. What you have will do just fine. This isn't the White House, Tapscott."

With that and a forceful tug of the elbow, Alton Tapscott was abducted from his morning's comfort, wearing nothing but his plaid red robe, plaid green boxers, and a white T-shirt. No slippers.

*****

There was the sense of a general pace stirring about the hallways of the clubhouse. Orderlies moved residents in wheelchairs on the right side, curving around wet floor signs, and others walked determined toward the dining hall. The sound of rayon rubbing from the left side mixed with the squawk of chair legs dragging on the wooden floors.

"Don't get too dressed up on your first day or nuthin, Tapscott," E.B. snickered.

"Shut it, E.B. Did you reserve our table?" Murray said as he scurried toward the room, a slight scowl on his face. When Murray made the turn into the dining hall, the fluorescent glow of the room sat on his face and made his reddish hair almost translucent. "Good morning, everybody!" Murray called, before stepping into the light.

"Don't pay mind to Mr. Murray being in such a rush. He likes to get in there and hob-nob before the fun starts, that's all."

"They don't show you all this in the nursing home's flier," Tapscott said, watching the traffic of walkers and chairs merge into the door frame.

"It's a retirement community, Tap-scott. Come on, I'll introduce you to the room."

His stomach jumped at the prospect of meeting an entire room, let alone on the arm of E.B. Falgoust.

The breakfast rush was over, and the dietary staff had transformed the dining hall into a full-fledged, state-of-the-art bingo hall. They'd removed the tablecloths and wheeled in the wired hamster dome. The decaf they kept flowing. The sun didn't come through the lace curtains until the afternoon, so the soft buzz of fluorescent lighting met them at the door.

Residents sat four to a table, three if a wheelchair pulled up. Tapscott sat at the head table with Murray, E.B., and the wired hamster wheel that E.B. claimed was St. Ignatius' first order from a drone delivery service decades earlier. The younger residents scooted in, shouting idle threats of the homes they'd buy or places they'd go with the bounty of the game. The older people, the geezers, followed with stooped backs, sore elbows, and knotted ankles as thick as a tree limb.

He felt his index and thumb careening toward the bridge of his nose when Samantha's voice boomed over a microphone, "Good morning, Saint Ignatius residents!"

The room was silent except for the faint shriek of what many assumed to be a squirrel, which wound up being Mr. Kershaw setting his hearing aid past the doctor's recommended auditory dosage.

"Okay, everyone. We can do better than that."

"Oh, not this," Tapscott whispered to himself.

"I said, good morning!"

The crowd's murmur reached the fevered pitch of a group watching a hotly contested croquet match.

"Okay, that's better." She smiled. "So, before we get started, Mr. Murray has something he'd like to say."

Murray stood, pressing the front of his shirt and slacks in one motion like he'd just stole second base.

"Everybody, listen up!"

The sound of E.B.'s voice produced a noticeable wince from the crowd. His smile indicated he was pleasantly surprised by the reaction, but four feet to his left, Murray was staring a hole through Mr. Falgoust's forehead.

E.B., unaware or undaunted, continued, "The board president is speaking!"

"Now, that will be quite enough, Mr. Falgoust!" Murray's blood cells gathered at his cheeks, his face as red as a hornet sting. A wave of wrinkles swept over the red sea of his face, and with pursed lips, he motioned for E.B. to take a seat. "We have a new resident with us today. No doubt, some of you met him on his tour. Everyone, help me welcome Professor Alton Tap-scott!"

Tapscott glanced around the room, nodding at any eyes that came to meet his, but most were busy organizing their plastic red, blue, and white poker chip bingo markers.

"He's taking over Sylvia's spot in the back. So, let's welcome Professor Scott … Tapscott. Stand up, Alton!"

He stood, leaning on his walker, lifting one stiff arm to wave before lowering back to the chair. All the pleasantries, out of breath.

"Okay, okay," E.B. Falgoust cut through the confused crowd, "let's get this show on the road."

After a rousing round of personal intentions during morning prayer, where Mr. Ian Wyble prayed for his grandkids that hadn't come to see him in eighteen months, Mr. Toby Richard prayed for the military that hadn't sent his V.A. check on time in two years, and Mr. Joe Womack prayed for the president whose name escaped him for the time, Samantha passed out the cards. Four cardboard bingo cards were placed neatly in front of the residents in a square. Some of the boards possessed built-in sliding plastic markers.

"Everybody ready?"

"No!" shouted a voice from the back.

"Dammit, Cliff! Get your cards in order!" Murray shouted.

"He doesn't have chips yet," came a defense.

"Well, okay. Just say so, damn!" Murray puffed his chest and bobbed his head from side to side. He leaned down to Tapscott and whispered while nudging him with his elbow, "You see what we're dealing with up here?"

He was shaking his head enough that Tapscott felt his frustration and had that clenched jaw that people get when they're holding their tongue.

E.B.'s head joined the pair at the center of the table. "You see what we deal with around here? They're tryna get a rise outta Mr. Murray thas all."

Murray shot a glance at E.B. while Tapscott watched a woman, Mrs. Anne Renee, fumble with her poker chips. They slipped from her grasp and toppled, one over the other, to the white linoleum floor. Nobody seemed to notice her quiet eyes calling for help amidst the commotion of card distribution, residents shouting for different cards, and Murray dressing down E.B. She made no attempt to retrieve her markers. No effort to roll back her wheelchair. Others at her table hadn't noticed—studying their cards and stacking markers. An orderly walking by was having a conversation, either with himself or his LIZA. It reminded Tapscott of his first time falling in the shower. It was the beginning of the end for his independence. The longer his face pressed the white porcelain shower floor, the more he knew Archie would make a fuss. He crawled, climbed, and scratched his way across the bathroom to scream up at LIZA. She called for help. The E.M.T. crew was live-streaming the rescue for the local news. Instead of Archie finding his dad soaked in suds on the bathroom floor and delivering a lecture, the whole of south Louisiana would get to see it projected on their bedroom ceiling as they crawled, climbed, and scratched their way into bed that night. He'd embarrassed Archie in the public sphere for the last time.

"Isn't this sad?" Murray broke his concentration.

"Sad? Sorry, I'm not following."

"Just these people." Murray rolled his eyes. "Can't get them to show up for a resident council meeting or a disciplinary hearing, and they groan and moan their way into mass each week, but here they are. Ready to bite my head off for trying to get this show on the road."

"That woman at the table over there … she dropped some chips, it looks like."

"Anne Renee? Jesus Christ. There's no helpin' some."

"Yeah, she don't ever win anyway," E.B. chimed in.

"Well, she'd need chips to do that, right?" Tapscott meant this with all sincerity, but he saw his two compatriots were having none of it.

"It's bingo, Tap. The less competition, the better," Murray gruffed.

"Yeah, this is just simple numbers, Tapscott. Odds. You weren't a math professor, huh?" E.B. delivered his line with a slap on Tapscott's back.

"I see what you guys are talking about." Tapscott began to nod. "Yeah. They're all a bit uncivilized if you ask me."

"Exactly. Now you're gettin' it."

"Okay," Cooper cried. "Everybody ready now?"

"Ready!" responded in Marine-like unison.

"Okay, okay. First ball … first ball … B-5!" E.B. shouted as if a life raft was passing by. "B-5!"

He checked his four cards. No B-5.

But heard Murray whisper, "Yes. Yes. Keep 'em comin.'" Murray had three B-5s.

"G-49! G, as in Good. G-49!"

Three cards with G-49. He scrambled to throw markers down before the rattle of the ball's cage came to another stop.

"0-63! 0-63!"

Rattle. Rattle. Clank.

"B-12! B-12! If anyone got a deficiency, we've got your B-12!" E.B. held the ball over his head, surveying the room with a smile.

"I-29!"

A voice interrupted from the left side of the room, "I drove down 1-29 once."

Murray and E.B. pounced like a couple of kids on a stuffed crust pizza.

"That's enough, Zach!"

"Shut it, Zach!"

"Jesus! We're trying to play bingo, people! Christ!"

The sound of suppressed laughter emitted from the back left, which caused E.B. and Murray to find their feet in anger. Tapscott remained seated and a bit scared. His expression blank and head craned to the side to avoid any and all eye contact.

"Let's get it together, everybody. Stop the laughing. Stop the talking. If you can't behave, we won't play."

"See how funny you think that is," added E.B. "We'll shut this down like two months ago."

Murray settled back down, and the game kicked back into gear. Tapscott's eyes hadn't yet made it above the horizon of his top card.

"I-40!"

"*Bingo!* I got bingo!"

"We've got a bingo back here!"

"It's me!" A woman sat back in her chair and waved her card over her head. Her arm skin flapped as if she might take flight right out of her seat. "I've got a *bingo!*" It was Poppy Burt, and even though the thought of winning scared Tapscott half the death, he didn't want her taking any money either.

"Nobody move! Nobody move! We need to check her card." With the rush of a recently opened salad bar, Murray made his way back to the table. "Way to go, Poppy!" and other congratulatory calls sprouted out about the room.

"Quiet now. We've got to read them … B-5."

"Yes …"

"I-29."

"Yes."

"N-40."

"Okay."

"G-52."

"Well, now wait a minute, Ms. Poppy." E.B. was studying the balls in front of him. "I don't think I called B-5."

"Dammit, Falgoust!" came a call from the left. It was the deacon. He wasn't much of a gambling man, and his wife usually forced him to go to rosary during this time, but he made an exception for bingo. "Don't start this again."

"Hold your horses, Deacon," Murray said, motioning his hands in front of him like patting two large, invisible dogs. "Let's make sure we're fair here. Check the balls, E.B."

"Mr. Murray, I think Ms. Poppy must've misunderstood. I didn't say B-5, I said, 'Be qui-et!'"

Tapscott glanced at Murray's card, littered on the left side with B-5s.

"Now," Murray said, studying the card, "this is unfortunate. But, if you say so, E.B. Sorry, Ms. Poppy, rules is rules."

Somebody shouted for Samantha to come clear the air, but she was on her state-allotted thirty-minute break.

"Sorry, dear. Maybe it'll hit B-5 real soon!" Murray turned and pushed his way back to the front, raising to the tips of his Oxford shoes when he danced through a row of wheelchairs.

Back at the hamster wheel, E.B. began the process again. The chips on Murray's board hadn't moved in between bouts of nervous glances at the room and his bingo boards. All his B-5s still sat hidden from the rest of the room. Murray glanced over and winked.

"I-22!"

"Well, I'll be damned. I've driven down I-22!"

"Zach!"

"Dammit, Zach."

Pockets of laugher sprang out as the two venerable Bourgeoisie fought for peace and dignity in the St. Ignatius Retirement Community Bingo and Dining Hall. The laughter morphed into intense coughing, hacking, and gagging from the crowd. Tapscott fought back a smile. He, too, once drove down I-22 on a trip to Tupelo, Mississippi. Evelyn's soccer tournament or Archie's lacrosse game—it was one of the two and it was a desolate stretch with little GPS connection and even less pavement.

"All right!" Cooper bellowed. "Back on track ... again!"

"B-7! B-7"

"Bingo! Bingo! Bingo!" Murray was flailing his arms, laughing, cooing, cawing, leaning back and kicking his feet under the card table. "Finally! Y'all know I've been due long enough!"

"You won two days ago," said a voice from the back.

"Hey, quit that now!" E.B. looked as though his wife was dragged in front of a court and slapped. "No need for petty jealousy. Congratulate Mr. Murray or say nothin' at all."

The room lay silent.

"Nice job, Cooper," Tapscott whispered in his general direction.

"Read 'em off!" said a new voice. It was the custodian, Marlon. His smile caused his enormous tic-tac teeth to almost jump out his mouth. "Come on, Mr. E.B., you know the rules, now." Marlon leaned against a wheelchair handrail at the entrance, wiping his brow with a blue towel. His skin only enhanced his teal blue uniform that consisted of a short-sleeve button-up and pants.

These fleeting moments of what Tapscott imagined as the real world, existence outside of the walls of this home, came in spurts. Seeing Marlon's jovial grin reminded Tapscott this was a game. He was in a contest for five dollars, and the stupefying direction it'd taken was just that.

The quiet room sat, eyes fixed to E.B., Cooper, and, by association, Alton Tapscott.

Marlon burst into laughter. "Come on now, E.B. You know I'm just messin' with you. You're my boy, E.B."

A ghost must've snuck up on E.B. and lifted the sack of potatoes off his back. His proceeding laugh was equal parts exhale and chortle.

"Very funny, Marlon! Yes. Very funny indeed. Mr. Marlon, everybody!" Murray was gesturing to the audience like he was introducing a speaker at a convention. "Now, run along now. I know for certain the toilets in the Rec Hall need your undivided attention today."

Marlon waved to a few residents before leaving, a smile stapled to his face. "See y'all!" he shouted as he spun through the French doors behind him.

E.B. and Murray glanced at one another.

"Tap, just hope you don't have too many run-ins with Marlon Butler while you're here," Cooper said.

"He seemed like an all right guy."

"Seemed. That's the keyword there. He's all show. He thinks he's a comedian. I'm thinking about bringing him up at the next board meeting. There has to be better help in this town."

"Okay, Mr. Murray," E.B. introduced the rest of the room back into the conversation, "let's move right along. We've been at it for a while now and only played one game. Clear your cards, everybody. Clear your cards!"

Chips rained down on the card tables about the room. The commotion of rearranging chips, chairs, and chatter filled the room as game two commenced. Murray leaned forward and placed a small pencil pouch on the table.

"What's this?"

"It's your cut," whispered Murray. "Take it as a welcome to S.I. gift from me and E.B."

Tapscott hesitated. He'd never been paid off before, so this was an opportunity to try something new … Archie begged him to do that for years.

Hey, if you ain't cheatin', you ain't trying. Tapscott's uncle used to say that during card games. He would go on to steal money from almost everyone he knew and end up in federal prison.

*****

The clubhouse smelled of syrup and cigars, with the slight odor of dentures. The trio sat in the den, Murray's words fighting past the e-cigar in his teeth as he lay back in a leather armchair, all squinting to see the drama serial on the TV set.

"So, Tap-scott, what do you think of Ignatius so far?"

It was half-past eight p.m., and the boys had a full run of the grounds that day. They won bingo, placed bets on shuffleboard—fleeing in a golf cart after losing—and went to mass, but only for communion. Now half-drunk on the watered-down blood of Christ, they settled into blowing smoke.

"More importantly," Murray sat up before Tapscott answered, saying, "how do you like the company you're keeping here?" He leaned forward in the chair, creases in the old leather stretched and cracked.

Tapscott's eyes fixated on the billowing cloud of smoke rising to the popcorn ceiling. "Well, gentlemen," he said, smiling, "like this stogie and this scotch, I'd say the company has been cheap!"

The three clapped their hands to their respective knees and stomped like children snuffing out an ant colony, their eyes wet from the smoky air. "It's been an interesting day. That's for sure." Sensing more was needed, he added, "I appreciate you getting me out, Cooper."

"Don't make a scene, Tap-scott." Murray grinned and elbowed E.B. "We just wanted to show you the ropes. It can really be a top-notch retirement community, but to do that, you got to stop with the pity party and get away from the riffraff." Murray inhaled and muttered to himself, "Tap ... Scott. Tap. Scott. You really should think about changing that. It's a mouthful."

"Like that deacon," E.B. chimed in from the arm of Murray's chair. "Riffraff."

Tapscott felt the warmth of the cigar smoke working through

his throat, to his lungs, and to his belly. The sticky stench invaded his body, bushwhacking through the clutter and the clots. He was beginning to think inhaling the smoke was a bad idea.

After a lengthy court case in the 1990s, a Mississippi lawyer won a decision against what was then called big tobacco. The trial concluded that cigarette companies had to state the obvious—inhaling tar will, inevitably and most tellingly, kill you dead. It didn't make it any less delicious, and the people of Mississippi fought yellow tooth and nail to beat out Louisiana for the most cigarette-induced deaths since the ruling. The population got together and created e-cigarettes with fun flavors for kids, which were banned altogether in 2022. So, in 2032, when that same Mississippi lawyer's son took on what was now known as little tobacco, once again scoring a victory, the judge ruled tobacco was nonsense altogether. Smokable leaves were banned, and in their place crept the e-cigar companies, now known formally as electronic tobacco, or Big E.T. Everyone knew e-cigars were far worse than their agro-predecessors, which seemed like a health kick after one puff of their futuristic counterparts.

"AAAA-CKK! Ughh! AAAA-Ck!" It sounded like he was starting a chainsaw in his esophagus.

"Taps!" Murray lunged forward. "Don't die on your first week, ya big goof!" He slapped Tapscott on the back a few times. "Blink, Mister Tapscott. Blink and breathe."

Tapscott sat up, looking at the ceiling through tears in his eyes.

"Oh my. Damn!" He gave a wry smile at the two hyenas sitting on a chair across from him.

"You'll get the hang of it," Murray said, wiping away tears of his own.

"Yeah, he's not quite there yet, Cooper," E.B. said, smiling through the water in his eyelashes. "Hell, I still wake up feeling terrible the next day every time we do this," E.B. added.

"This can't be sanitary." Tapscott hacked again.

"Well, that's because these are sorry stogies," Murry said as he examined the $4.99 EL-Cubano in his hand. "My son, Gunnar, great kid." E.B. was nodding behind Murray in agreement. "But he gives me such a paltry allowance for nonessentials, bourbon and cigars, that I had to settle on Cubans for now. Strange to think these used to be a delicacy. You know, they still use the Cuban leaves for chewing."

"The real thing?" E.B. Falgoust asked.

"The real thing, I think," Murray said, twisting the e-cigar in his index and middle fingers. "Probably a hit somewhere less civilized. Like Missouri. I think that's where Camille is from. Or France. Taps, one of the things up here, and I've accepted this, I'm perfectly resigned being around people that don't read or reflect on anything, but I don't feel close to those people out there. And I can't quite come to grips with how they stand each other. They aren't intellectuals like us."

"In-tu-lect-tals," E.B. repeated.

"They've got no drive left. No sir. Nuthin. It's a damn shame."

"Damn shame," E.B. repeated.

E.B. ran home to his wife a little after nine, leaving Tapscott and Cooper to stay up half the night, running up the electricity bill, watching the TV as two local politicians battled over voting rights with a game of bowling. "He tells the truth," Cooper would say.

"But he's a better bowler," Tapscott replied.

"My son voted for him," Murray said. "Or least got drinks with him once."

Tapscott respected Cooper for moving on from his son. Finding a new calling, dusting himself off, and straightening out some of these characters up here. The pair were more alike than he'd first thought. Losing responsibility for your own life is a fate usually left for heinous convicts, but it is far too often assigned to the old or the perceived decrepit. It's hard to demand freedom from a soiled diaper ... it was why babies didn't run for public office. And they couldn't bowl.

People's lives sat out of reach, their own hands disabled by time or power of attorney. Some credited one of many higher powers, but others simply handed over their time in vain, giving up their equity in exchange for the numb, painless comfort of hospital gown. Their cards were on the table, but the next big thing was on TV. Not mindless, but apathy had a way of devouring over time and beating any disposition into submission. When his wife died, like a sedative suppository, Tapscott fell into living obscurity. The starch faded. Fate was waiting, but for too many a whimper echoes from their last moment.

CHAPTER 5

The droll pat of kitty litter awoke him on Saturday morning at the end of his first week. He'd missed five a.m. mass yet again. Emerging from the lavatories, Mack sunk his claws into the side of the mattress, working out any kinks in his shoulders.

"Well good morning!" Tapscott said, attempting to sit up. "Finished with your morning constitutional before breakfast, eh?"

With a leap, Mack floated to the foot of the mattress.

"Get over here you sack of—" He mustered all the forces of his ailing abdomen and lurched to grab the slippery cat. Mack bounced off the mattress and onto the dresser across the room, licking the fuzzy part between his crotch and legs.

"Never mind all that." Tapscott swung his legs in unison to the edge of the bed and used the spring of the mattress to vault himself upright to his walker. He'd picked up a few tricks from observing some of the batty men and women around the grounds this week. Some had a small satchel on their walkers, made it easier to carry the essentials: wallet, wet wipes, and a small mister. The middle bar made lugging a magazine or newspaper simple; just by folding it over the top, he'd present the image of a well-read man. He'd yet to solve a crossword puzzle in his life, but that didn't mean his walker shouldn't schlep one.

He dumped his belongings into this satchel and clanked into the kitchen. Mack trailed behind. "Coffee on! Now! Let's go!"

With water boiling and milk flowing into cup and bowl, he sat back on a stool and studied the pages of the *New York Times* Crossword booklet.

"*Expensive purchase with a distinctive smell …* six letters across … *Perfum*! Or is there an E at the end? I doubt it." He smiled. "Mack, my dear boy, I've never been a man for puzzles and games. There are enough tricks and turns in life, why bear out more stress on yourself than need be? But dammit if my mind isn't as sharp as always, these last few days. I think it's the company, to tell you the truth. I had, as you know, been spending my time emulating that of Milton or O'Connor, secluding myself to explore the greater reaches of the TV and radio. But dammit if I'm just too charming to stay locked away in that old house. This apartment suits us just fine. Don't you say?"

The cat sat, nose buried in a short saucer of milk, licking the top and creating a small wave against the tin. His eyes were closed, and he crouched into a tight ball as if you might throw him like a football. His whiskers dipped in and out of the milk as he adjusted the pads of his feet on the cold tile kitchen floor.

"Well look who I'm talking to. You're an orphan. Six letters across, *easy baseball outs … Easy baseball outs … Easy baseball outs …* a pop up! Of course. I really should take you to a game. You know I was something of an athlete of sorts in my day, Mack. Really was." He squinted and drew in each letter of pop ups. "I did it all. I hit, I pitched, I caught, I threw, I squashed the bug and ran the bases. But that was all before you knew me. Before I turned eighteen." He pulled his boxers up and around his gut, tightening around his navel.

"I've sought counsel with Murray and E.B. on a few occasions this week. There really are a strange lot around us here. Murray is sure I'll be able to find refuge near his condo at the front of the property soon." Tapscott turned on one heel and leaned the small of his back against the top of the kitchen counter.

The coffee pot rumbled, spurting down hot, brown liquid into a small, white cup. He tried to pick it up, but the drops singed his knuckle-hair when his hand went for the mug. He opened a few drawers but couldn't find a proper rag to wrap his finger, so he used his robe.

"The pit of undesirables we've landed in on this block isn't good for my assimilation to this lifestyle, I explained to the director of the property this week. His lord graced us with his presence at the resident council meeting on Thursday. You shoulda seen him, on his phone, never once looking up to hear some of the real issues about the place. And that Burt woman. If I hear one more smooth-brained theory about the council elections being rigged or counted incorrectly again, dammit I'll have to up the dose on my diuretics!"

Mack hopped down from the counter and scampered to his spot on the monkey chair.

Whiskers of gray and diluted brown colonized Tapscott's face as never before. There, in the soft glow of morning and fluorescent kitchen light, tufts of shirt sprung forth from his red and white checkered boxers. His knees held steady and back stiffened with each sip of coffee. His skin was not yet bruised and swollen like some of the patrons in this place, eyes were still observant. His white shirt came from an online salesman years before, the restrictions of true pajamas too much to handle. The pleats on his boxers were man-made and provided room for agility and comfort. A sensible outfit for one's house, he announced, spotting the blotches of coffee, milk, and cranberry juice about his shirt.

He'd become frustrated by his puzzle, a rather mundane clue "Soap bubbles" made him toss it aside.

"Now why do they do this, Mack?" he started in. "I have half a mind to write to these people. Of course, they don't provide an email address for complaints. How convenient! Nobody wants to hear about anyone else's problems anymore. I, myself, as you know, have deep convictions concerning social injustices in this country. I cannot sit idly by while some nitwit in New York City gets paid a livable wage to perpetrate such faulty notions of academia and knowledge. Soap bubbles! What kind of a clue is that? This just won't … do …"

He scrambled through the kitchen drawers for pen and paper. If he failed to jot this diatribe down now, who knows who might miss hearing it later? The thought of sending an email to his old friend and associate across town, Charles Logan, popped in his mind, but a person his age out in the free world on his own, not being looked after only depressed Tapscott. Besides, it wasn't real depression—he was just apprehensive to the idea everyone else had it better than he did.

"I have a notion… that I was created on the wrong side of equal," he said to the cat.

Mack sat upright on his front paws with his hind legs shooting up toward the ceiling as he scooted along the thick, bristled carpet in the living room emitting a soft noise with each skid. His back facing the sun in the courtyard, the residents of St. Ignatius growling to the day's start.

*****

The crash of characters Tapscott came to know attended each event at the condo community. Bingo, Pokeno, tennis, nail painting, and even casino night. He and Cooper didn't avoid their stares but soaked in them. At the weekly silent retreat, it came to such a head that the pair escaped to the convent's movie theater via golf cart to avoid both participation and perspiration.

"A little silence will do that lot good," Cooper surmised. "We'd be better suited elsewhere."

There was a man—a big, rhinoceros of a man—rolled into the dining hall out of the sweltering heat in a silver and blue wheelchair with wheels so worse for wear that Tapscott heard him before seeing him. His dark hair and skin melted into his faded black and purple track suit, and his back somehow spilled out of the rear of his pants and chair. His whole body gave off the feeling it might burst at the slightest prick of the insulin needle. Behind a pair of sunglasses, his dark eyes danced about the room, scanning for any sign of life. They targeted and passed over the lump that was Alton Tapscott.

"You can't help some people." Murray said. "We try to include him. Try to make others feel welcome, but this guy won't get up off his ass to greet newcomers or a soul." E.B. noted he didn't think he had the physical ability to stand up. Murray brushed it off as poor effort.

His name was Noel Cone, E.B. explained, and he was probably there to see his daughter. Tapscott figured he knew him well enough just from the television channels he heard through the walls.

Mr. Cone brushed past the talking heads on the way to an empty table. A paper bag sat folded, at the top a white note stapled. He studied the note, took the bag in his lap, and crept out of the dining hall.

Tapscott didn't see him again for four days until he noticed someone under one of the stations of the cross on the walking path while Cooper and Tapscott buzzed by on a golf cart, a large clump of a man bumping over the rocks and the roots somewhere around Jesus' third fall.

A day after that, Cone's TV went silent for the first time since Tapscott was thrown into his room.

"What do you think is going on over there, Mack?" He opened the front door to peer out, then the back. Nothing. Exhausted from his investigative work, he pulled up a chair and pressed his ear against the wall, this time with more force, and adjusted it every so often like a pillow until he was fast asleep in his apartment bathroom, his face periodically squeaking against the wall as it slid down to its resting place.

*****

On the other side of the wall, he heard the elephantine figure swish over linoleum floors, almost hovering from room to room. Tapscott heard cooking. A woman's voice sang.

"Happy anniversary, honey!" said the female voice.

"*Take the previously separated egg yolk,*" a robotic sound called out.

"Can you believe it's been forty-four years?" the woman continued.

"*Slowly stir it into the pasta.*"

The whir of a Joy for All Scottish terrier was close to the wall, Tapscott thought. He heard the springs of a Laz-E-Boy shoot into action.

"I love you, Noel. I hope you like your e-card."

*****

Bugs swarmed out by the fountain. The heavy air and soft flow of the apartments' porch lights attracted flocks of mosquitos. Poppy Burt's porch light doubled as a zapper, so anyone darkening her doorstep the following morning would announce themselves with the damp crunch of gnat carcasses. She sent an email each morning to the community director complaining that the housekeeping staff wasn't quick enough to her "side of the estate" and she wasn't paying good money to see dead bugs and cicada shells. Cooper Murray didn't tell her Medicare was footing the bill so long as her foot didn't heal.

A condo block down from Tapscott, apartment 3B's light twinkled in the muggy night. Water sat on the viridescent bulb like a moist glue and the condensation infiltrated the electrical wiring. A low hum proceeded the loud *zap* and *pop*. The light went out on apartment 3B's porch, and the bugs fought through the humidity to find another home.

CHAPTER 6

Two parallel lines formed in the courtyard; a lethargic game of red rover was about to start. Murray and E.B. had shaken Tapscott from his sleep, and he stood out in the heat, confused and on the verge of arousal, in his boxers and sleep shirt. The milky light seeped through the dense wetness of the morning.

"What is going on? Why is nobody speaking?" he whispered.

"We are about to find out," E.B. answered. "This'll be your first one."

"First what? And why can't I have shorts on for this?"

"You two hush. It's disrespectful. This one hits home for me. He was a walkie-talkie after all, not some nursing wing vegetable," Murray grunted. Murray was in a starched nightgown with satin blue piping down the sides. His initials sat on his left breast pocket in bright white thread and his house slippers were a rich dark red.

E.B. shot a glance at Tapscott, whose eyebrows hadn't come to rest since he was pushed onto the concrete courtyard two minutes before. At the other end, a table began rolling into view. A troop of five men in dark blue scrubs asked for space to get through. An orderly sprang into action, e-cigarette at his lips, to pull a chair bound resident out of the way. The men whisked by as the table's wheels clanked and stumbled over the cracks of the concrete.

"Please make room! Thank you!" one of the men called.

"Make some room, people!" E.B. echoed. "Wake up!"

A light blue, almost white sheet rippled in the wind as the men shuffled by Tapscott's porch. With a short gust, a small, pasty white foot came into view under the sheet as it bounced along. At one point they hit a bump that almost did in the entire operation. The men began to shout until Murray and E.B. decided they better go oversee the situation.

Tapscott began to accompany the group until noticing the stillness of other residents. The frozen line, the Kirbys, the Rudolphs, the Wybles, Mr. Majoria and Mr. Romero all sat still as can be, staring at invisible targets somewhere on the ground. He scanned the ground for anything of interest. It was then he noticed a large shadow growing at his feet, stretching beyond almost to the fountain. He turned, trying to make eye contact for a subtle shoulder shrug or head nod, but Mr. Cone--whose shadow was now blocking the sun entirely--was wearing his usual sunglasses, so Tapscott ended up shaking his upper body as if he had an itch.

And there everyone sat and stood, the weather hot and the mood drenched in eerie anticipation. Perhaps more for the morbid knowledge that their clock was ticking than dignity for the dead, everyone was out. The crippling silence and voyeurism had Tapscott asking himself "How will I go?" and "Would I want to go out like that" and "E.B. better not wake anybody up to see me." And what age would I've liked to go? He'd passed that a while back, he thought. Before the hemorrhoids."

There was no movement in the courtyard until Mr. Cone swiveled his chair ninety degrees in an instant, and with a great puff, another ninety, until he was facing his door again. Tapscott decided now was his chance to make a good first impression.

"Did you catch the show last night?" he blurted out, a voice in his head shouting to lower his voice. He stared at the large back.

Mr. Cone's head tilted up until his face appeared in the reflection of his apartment's glass door. His tawny skin reflected the light off high cheekbones and a pair of bruised but tame eyebrows, smooth but curved, perched over the rim of his dark glasses. Mr. Cone turned his wheelchair a bit, his right ear facing Tapscott, while he craned his neck and head.

"Did you mean me?" Mr. Cone asked.

"Well, yeah. Did you catch the episode of *Celebrity Olympics*? I heard you watching it last week—"

Noel Cone shook his head. His nose scrunched to the bridge of his sunglasses as if he smelled something unfamiliar, and his nod was slow and short enough that it made him look more confused than in disagreement.

"No. I didn't catch the episode."

"Well, okay. For whatever reason I thought you were a fan."

"Are you surveilling me, Mr. Tapscott?"

"Surveil— No! Of course not." Tapscott laughed, then lowered his voice and glanced around the courtyard. "Um, no, of course not. I can just hear through the wall. Can't you hear me sometimes?"

"I can, but that doesn't mean that I do. Unless you're talking to your son, of course." Noel gave the inkling of a smile, and Tapscott caught a glimmer of bright white teeth swallowed by the enlarged cheeks and lips.

"Oh, Archie. Yeah. He's a good kid, really. Just not always available, I guess. He's got kids. He's busy."

"Hey, you don't have to explain it to me. Everybody up here's got some of that going on. Yes, indeed."

Doors creaked open all around the courtyard now, the spring-loaded screen doors slammed, others with a soft clang of the metal frame, shut behind their owners until it was only him and Noel Cone looking at one another.

"So," Tapscott broke the silence, "what was all this about? Cooper and E.B. got me up for this, or else I'd be dressed at least in some khaki shorts, ya know?" His nervous cackle was cut short by a coughing fit.

"Well, it looks like Mr. Doug in 3B passed last night. I heard

the maintenance man came to fix his light this morning and
looked in. He was on the ground apparently." Noel shifted in his
chair— his arms picked up his entire bodyweight like he'd placed
bronze in the pommel horse. "On the floor and piss running
down his leg. No way to go."

"What a shame. How'd everyone hear about it so fast?"

"Oh, Marlon came running through here screaming like
a damn fool. The night nurse had probably left, so there was a
ruckus getting him up and checked out. They call an ambulance
every time, but I don't know why. If he's dead enough to get the
sheet, doesn't matter if he's on a stretcher or a wheelchair if you
ask me."

"Boy that'd be a sight," Tapscott said.

"Was," Noel said as he woofed up a cough that shook his
entire torso. "Was a sight. That's how they took my Cora out of
here. Head bobbing, arms limp. Just rolled her on out."

After raising a couple of kids through the age of social media,
Tapscott knew well the idiom that it was sometimes best to say
nothing at all. Like many of a certain age, his instincts and actions
weren't harmoniously aligned.

"Like *Weekend at Bernie's*?"

Noel's lips parted for a moment, and his stark white teeth
shone through to Alton Tapscott's aging eyes. From his molars to
his incisors, his teeth sat on red and blue gums like shining oyster
pearls on a fish's tongue. His laughter shook the shingles on the
two men's apartment building. His gut bobbed up and down as if
his intestines were punching from within. Noel stood up in one
swift move, and the mass of a man patted Tapscott on the back
while, with a single hand, picked up and folded his wheelchair.
He towered over Tapscott's head, high enough to probably see
the marks from a few benign moles.

"Yes, sir. Yes, sir. Like that movie. I guess I hadn't really seen the humor in the whole situation, with it being my wife."

Tapscott felt his breath leave him for a moment as he closed his eyes and thought about running back into his apartment. When you meet someone who's experienced loss, his mother used to tell him, you have two options: one is to say you're sorry, the other is to share in it. But like an office birthday, if nobody knows beforehand, it's uncouth to spontaneously announce it yourself, so he kept his grief to himself.

"I'm sorry, Mr. Cone. I–I didn't mean it to be funny." He searched for his next words. "But doesn't seem dignified, does it?"

"Sure didn't at the time, Mr. Tapscott. And you can call me Noel ... Alton, right?

"No, Tapscott is fine."

"What about yours--you have a wife or..."

"Oh, no, I did," Tapscott said. "She, uh, she passed a couple of years ago. Got hit by one of those AI-driven grocery store karts while returning hers to the stall. Right in the middle of the parking lot. It was about the last time I could stomach common courtesy like that. Or groceries"

"Oh, no indeed. Did you sign the waiver? You didn't did you?"

"We'd signed the waiver--so no wrongful death or anything. My friend looked into it for me."

"Well, Tap-scott, people our age, we're used to undignified situations a little bit, aren't we? Or maybe I'm a fast learner." Noel was shaking his head.

"That's the worst thing about this place," Tapscott said, "The indignity. It'd be fine if I could at least talk to her about it. She'd have a laugh. But now that she's gone, I feel like I didn't look at her enough. Can't remember what she sounded like sometimes. That's

what I miss the most." He shook his head, remembering where
he was. "But hey--I'll let Cooper know about your wife--Cora.
He and I are close, and if I say something, he'll bring it up to the
board, I'm sure—maybe get a gift basket or something out of it?"

Noel's smile faded, then grew and doubled in size as Tapscott
spoke. "That's just unacceptable. Unacceptable. A gift basket is
the least they could do."

"Oh, yes. Tell Cooper Murray you spoke with me. Tell him
you spoke with Noel Cone. I'd be happy to hear what his thoughts
are on the little blunder we had over here. Yes, indeed."

"Mr. Cone … I mean, Noel, I promise I'll bring it up. If you
want me to, that is."

"I don't think it will do much, but you're more than welcome
to try." With this, Noel began to turn back to his apartment door.

"When did all this happen with your wife, anyway?" he asked
as his neighbor was moments from shutting the door behind him.

"Oh, let's say about fifteen or sixteen days ago. Succeeded in
dying peacefully," he answered, head cocked toward the ground.

"Right before I got here? I'm sorry I didn't get to meet her.
Are you still living with all of her things? I know E.B. can sell
some furniture for you if you want to clear some room?" "Oh, she
didn't live in the apartment with me." Noel turned his big neck a
bit to right and nodded. "She lived in your spot. Moved her out
in a hurry. Yes, indeed. Have to move 'em quick if you want to
make money in this business—they had the contract signed on
someone new already—that's what I was told. Yes, indeed." There
was a slight pause before Noel asked, "How do you want to go?"

"From St. Ignatius?" Tapscott replied.

"No. From *here*," Noel said, shrugging, motioning to the sky.

"Louisiana?" Tapscott said, contemplating what'd kept him
there for so long. The natural disaster rate was the worst in the

country, the people were about as ambitious as an upturned turtle, and the Mexican food was lousy. But Baton Rouge was made for him—not New Orleans but far from Shreveport or, God forbid, the paved suburban Dallas where his cousins moved decades before to eat more steak or something. No, Baton Rouge had the perfect sense to ward away any threat of capable industry like manufacturing despite the schools' STEM curriculum which left Tapscott out of a job. His blood pressure might be lower somewhere with fewer fried shrimp options, but the stress of a move might've shot it through the roof straight into hypertension. It was a pickle. "I don't know what's keeping me here, really. We have the second-best water in the country behind Denver, right? Denver," he laughed, "what an erroneous assortment of scooters and millennial transplants."

"No, no. I'm talking about Earth, life, man." Noel laughed.

Tapscott paused, still half in thought about a margarita and half thinking about his death. "I didn't know I needed to plan that far ahead. I guess with some dignity?"

Noel smiled.

"How did you get over it? Move on?" Tapscott asked.

"The indignity or the death?"

"Both, I guess. I'm still trying."

Noel tapped his right ear, its lobe dropping passed his jawline. "My LIZA has a meditation app built in … did wonders. It's called glimpsing mindfulness. Or maybe mindful glimpsing? It's a Buddhist thing one of the kids showed me. Total clarity some days."

"Oh, I wasn't expecting that for some reason. And how long does it take you to reach total clarity? Or how many sessions? Is it a monthly prescription?"

"Total clarity? That's just about twenty minutes."

Tapscott shook his head. "Never mind then. I just don't know where anybody finds the time anymore."

Noel laughed a booming sort of chuckle that made his chest heave. "Good luck to you, Tapscott." He slipped inside of his dark apartment, looking back for a moment. "And watch out for Cooper Murray."

Tapscott's thoughts went to Noel's dead wife. He knew someone, sometime must've fallen or slipped or cut themselves in his apartment. But died? Passed on? Kicked the bucket? In *his* apartment? Where? The bedroom? This was a retirement community not a nursing home. Thoughts sprinted through his mind as Noel shut the door behind him, leaving Alton Tapscott alone in the courtyard, sweat running down his leg.

CHAPTER 7

A man in turquoise scrubs came to the apartment door later in the afternoon. Tapscott noticed a small figure blocking out the light from the front window and opened one blind to see a man with a pale stethoscope around his neck. Some edges frayed around the sleeves and cuffs, and, being the son of a physician, Tapscott knew that was the calling card of a lazy, good for nothing. He studied him further, squinting through the open slit.

"Excuse me?" the man said. "Mr. Tapscott? I'm looking for Mr. Tap … Scott 1B. You have a monthly check up."

"I only get checked by Dr. Addison," Tapscott spat. "And he doesn't usually see patients after noon, so—"

"I am the S.I. medical director, Mr. Tapscott." He glanced over Alton as, through measured pause and a palpable hangover, he read off a series of questions.

"Do you know what day it is?"

"Do I know what day it is?"

"Yes. Can you hear me okay?"

"I can hear you, but I don't understand the question."

"Okay, that's fine. Just tell me what you do and do not understand."

"No, I get the question."

"So, you do understand the question then? What is today?"

"That's a good question! What is today?" Tapscott shouted, loud enough he hoped that LIZA would hear.

"*Today is Tuesday. National Onion Rings Day.*"

"Why, today is Tuesday, Doctor!"

"Okay … wow." He shook his head. "Thank you for the enthusiasm." He was scribbling on a small, white notepad. "I'm going to tell you three words. See if you can repeat them back to me. Sock. Blue. Bay-d."

"Head?"

"No. The thing you lay on."

"Okay. Sock, blue, bed."

"Wait 'til I ask you later."

Tapscott glanced around, looking at his feet, then the doctor's. The man was wearing boots, which struck Tapscott as odd, since boots weren't a common occurrence within the city limits, and because he assumed any doctor would be on their feet too much to want such a clunky option. The leather was worn around the toes, the drooping sides of the foot covering the black soles.

"Do you wear boots every day?" he asked.

"Only when I'm working," the doctor mumbled. He scribbled then glanced over Tapscott one more time. "Okay," he paused, jerking his head up and again scanning as if he might catch a symptom if he surprised it, "let's get moving. I'll finish this up another time."

"Some check-up," Tapscott said. "Hope I did okay."

"You did fine, but we've got to be moving along. They're waiting on you in the den."

"The den?" Tapscott asked.

"I dunno, man," the doctor said. "They said to get a quick check-up, then escort you to the den."

The medical profession was too clerical these days. He wanted to bring this sloppy discourse up at the next resident council.

*****

"Do you know why you've been summoned, Mr. Tap ... scott?"

Six figures sat behind three conjoined folding tables placed adjacent to the clubhouse den's fireplace, their eyes fixed on a man, Tapscott, in the center of the room with a Simpson's medical-grade, two-button, folding walker, cabernet red. White tablecloths covered the tables' white tops but fell short of hiding the gray plastic legs—relinquishing all airs the ceremony might have born. The cloths were upside down in an apparent attempt to hide the tiny red and pink hearts embroidered around the edges, but they snuck into view as the corners jutted out like cowlicks. The disciplinary board meetings got the coarse white underside, and Valentine's Day celebrations got the rosy sheen on top.

Of the six figures, Tapscott made out only a few faces in the reflection of their tablet screens' glow. The dull screen light sat on their faces so that their foreheads and cheeks looked dark cliffs as they hunched over. Tapscott couldn't find the figure that had spoken, but none were making eye contact, so he decided to address the middle figure … who sat stiff and a bit larger than the rest.

"Well, Cooper told me—" His heart thumped in his ears, and the beat only grew louder after his voice came out with more of a tremble than he'd anticipated.

"Do you mean Mr. Murray?" came another voice.

"Well, yes, of course."

"Please note in the record Mr. Tapscott is referring to the board members by their first names," said the first voice.

"Well, hey now, Coop—er—Mr. Murray is the only one of you lot I've met so far."

"That's right, Mr. Tapscott," said the stiff, broad man in the middle. Reading glasses teetered on the tip of his nose as warm smile appeared. The man leaned back in his wooden armchair. "You really haven't been in here too long, have you?"

"A week tomorrow."

"We usually wait until at least the thirty-day doctor's check-up to hear from our newer residents, but here you are."

"Here I am, indeed! Where am I?"

"Do you *want* to be here, Mr. Tapscott?" The voice came from the opposite side of the plastic banquet, the tone more accusatory than the question might customarily require. The large man with a large voice. His brow hunched over his eye sockets, pen in his hand at the ready, looking like this was his chance to get to the scoop. He stared with the aggressive curiosity you might observe a passing plate of fajitas.

"This meeting?" Tapscott said with a tad of sincerity. "No. I'd rather not be. St. Ignatius, however, has been adequate so far. Exceeded my previously limited expectations, if you will."

"That's nice," one at the end said.

"I guess where we get confused is why you thought this would be a good idea. Aren't you eighty-two?" asked the broad-shouldered man.

"I am, but—"

"Well, this is not normal behavior for an eighty-two year old. You'll agree?"

Tapscott gave a hesitant nod to hint his confusion but cooperation.

"So maybe we're looking at an anger issue?" The two speakers leaned forward to get a better view of each other's approving eyes, nodding in intervals.

Tapscott shifted in his seat. "Now, I wouldn't say—"

"See, that's the thing, Mr. Tapscott. You didn't seem to have anything to say on the incident report you were given. That, according to the bylaws of this facility, is your time to voice your opinion. This is merely a fact-finding sentencing hearing."

"The incident report? Cooper told me—"

"Mister. Murray."

"Right, yes. Mr. Murray. He told me not to worry about the form. I could answer any questions here if the meeting was called."

Murray huddled at the edge of the last table, chair pulled up to the end in a seemingly last-ditch effort to join the fray. He sighed when the others looked at him, as his eyebrows, shoulders, and hands jumped to a confused shrug.

"Yeah, I'm not buying that."

"I'm not selling anything."

A third man in a plaid yellow shirt and sherbet tie broke into the mix, "You seem nervous, Mr. Tapscott. You aren't in trouble. There's no reason to spin a web to us here."

"I'm not selling or spinning. Haven't spun for years due to my friend here." Alton patted his walker and waited for a snort of laughter. He turned his auditory aid up after not hearing any.

"So, are we to understand you think what you did was reasonable?"

"Again, I'm not entirely sure—"

"We have other witnesses, Tapscott."

"Well, I could be a witness as well. Just let me know what we're talking about, and I'll spill."

Each member, save Cooper Murray, went to writing on his respective pad, eyes glued to the glow of the WriteWayz, a device which allowed the user to scribble on his personal pad then convert any writing to text and send to the group. It was developed to optimize office communication, but, like most communication devices, it was infested by bugs that hindered any real chance for the WriteWayz of overtaking conversation. Its biggest default was the font couldn't be altered from its original Cambria setting.

"You see, the Tapscotts aren't spinners or sellers, but I come from a long line of spillers."

"That's nice."

"Cody! Cody. Did you see this?" A quiet man at the end of the third table leaned back in a folding chair to the point it almost tipped and showed his screen to the hunched-brow man. His eyes lit up and head scrunched back into his neck like an ostrich staring down a corn cobb.

"I did not but thank God you showed me. Jesus."

"They're paying him that much to hit a baseball? Where did we go wrong?"

"Excuse me." Tapscott inched to the edge of his seat. "Listen, Cooper was there … he can tell you what, if anything, happened."

The room seemed to brighten when the row of men glanced up, screens reflecting in their glasses.

"Last warning, Mr. Tapscott. You will address the board respectfully or not at all. This hearing is a gift to you. This is not a right according to bylaw seventeen—"

"A gift? What bureaucratic red tape contest did I win?"

"Alton! Please!" Cooper Murray said, his hair disheveled with the violence of his neck movement. He stared wild-eyed at Tapscott.

"Yes," a member of the panel said, "a gift. Mr. Murray has gone to great lengths to ensure we hear your case. This process would normally not involve your participation, as I'm sure you can see at this point, but for a walkie-talkie like yourself, we thought you might be able to explain a bit."

"Are you seeing the same pattern we are, Mr. Tapscott?"

"You haven't been here a week and already in front of the board."

"You don't seem to respect the rules we've established here at St. Ignatius. Rules that have kept the people of this community safe and healthy for years."

"We're not saying you're a bad person."

A general chorus rang out in agreement.

"No, not a bad guy we don't think."

"Just maybe not the right person … not a good fit for this community."

The kitchen door creaked as it swung open, and Archie slipped in the room. He nodded toward Cooper and the board before shaking a few hands at the back. Murray jumped up to greet him.

"As I've said, I'm just having a little trouble nailing down exactly what went awry … yesterday? The day before? I don't even know the time and date!"

"And therein lies the problem."

"Yes. Lies. We feel you're too smart not to understand the situation, Tapscott. Either you're deceiving the board or not as sharp as you once were. Both are issues we must consider."

"As sharp as I once was? I was a community college instructor! Privileged in education and degrees, not in brains, I assure you!"

"But you introduced yourself as a professor, did you not?"

"That was a joke. A touch of deprecating irony."

"There you go again. A man of this vocabulary doesn't just forget his actions. Your file mentions nothing about memory loss. You were correct, Murray."

His eyes fought the darkness, looking for Murray. He heard whispering, and, with the auditory aid at full blast, heard the recognizable grunt of his son.

"I'm not a liar, and I don't have a memory issue. And how did you get my medical file?"

"The board is allowed access to medical files in the case of behavior issues for safety reasons, Mr. Tapscott. Bylaw 117. You should have read the rules and expectations of this community before moving in ... or did Mr. Murray tell you not to worry about that either?"

"Look, gentlemen," interrupted Cooper Murray from the back. He strode toward the dais, his long steps and red rubber soles bouncing across the floor. The loveseat's high winged back acted as polyester blinders and didn't afford Alton a chance at his peripherals, but the slush of newly purchased topsider boat shoes was undeniable. "I'd be willing to watch after Mr. Tapscott if he'd be willing to get some help."

"An honorable sentiment," it was agreed.

"With your current schedule, Murray? Honorable indeed."

"Help with what? My laundry?" Tapscott leaned forward to grasp the handles of his walker. A sign of action equivalent to a policeman unclipping his piece, although a walker somehow takes more effort. "I don't need help."

"Your anger, Alton. Your anger."

"I think I'm supposed to be Mr. Tapscott during this hearing."

"Now that's enough of the sarcasm," the big one said. "Quite frankly, I'm surprised you're not a bit grateful to Mr. Murray."

"*Grateful*?"

"Grateful."

"I assure you, my father is certainly grateful to be at St. Ignatius. I think you'll see a drastic change after a therapy session or two." Archie appeared at Alton's side. One hand scratching the back of his own head, the other on top of the winged chair. "Or twenty!"

The men of the board let out a hearty laugh in unison.

"Well, it's nice to see you, Archer. Glad you could find time in your busy—"

"Now, see. No!" Mr. Hunched Brow wagged a short index finger at Mr. Tapscott. "I just can't deal with this type of disrespect anymore."

"I agree. Show an ounce of appreciation for your son." The large man in glasses gave the plastic table an abrupt smack of frustration. "He's here on your behalf, by the way."

"He came to make sure I stay! So he doesn't have to take me."

"Let the record show Mr. Tapscott is raising his voice … unprovoked!"

"Let the record show Mr. Tapscott is not raising his voice!" cried Alton.

"Dad!"

"Enough is enough. You've been disrespectful since you came into the hearing, and this board is surprised after your actions the first day."

"Striking poor Mr. Marlon with your walker."

"You didn't have to hit him, Alton," Cooper said while looking at the floor.

"I apologized for all that. He said he understood I was under a lot of stress and angry my son had just … he understood. We've been cordial ever since! Chums, almost!"

"Ah! Angry. So, you're owning up to it?"

"Let's talk about what we can do to fix the problem, gentlemen," Archie broke in. "How do we stay proactive?"

"Well, I'd say due to the pattern of disobedience and delinquency exhibited by your father, we need to nip this in the bud quickly. What do you suggest, Mr. Tapscott?"

Alton began to speak but realized Archie was addressed in his place. His son, that he named, whose diapers he'd changed and who he'd taken to school and sent to college, toasted at his wedding, that baby was in charge now.

"I'll leave it up to the board. Y'all have more experience in matters like this, for sure," Archie said.

"Thank you, Mr. Tapscott. I think bi-weekly therapy visits would be appropriate."

"Second!"

"Therapy?" said Tapscott. His elbows dropped from parallel to below his walker handles. The triple threat position was no more.

"Your insurance will cover it. And the inevitable medications."

"Now, I don't think medications are necessary."

"You'll take them, or you won't be here, Mr. Tapscott. We've seen this problem in the past, and we like to fix it before it disrupts daily life at St. Ignatius."

"It won't be much, Mr. Tapscott. Just something to calm you down while you get acclimated to a new normal."

"What you're going through is common."

"But I'm not responding to this ambush reasonably?"

"Bingo!"

"Look at you, you're coming around to it already."

"So, this is it? I have to attend some looney toons sessions each week?"

The board members coiled, ready to strike out when Murray like a belching llama, choking a bit before thumping his chest clear of any blockage. "Tapscott, I would not call Sister Mary Clotilde's sessions looney toons. She is an accomplished therapist and godly woman."

"Second! Meeting adjourned? Minutes recorded?"

Papers shuffled here and there, and the men powered their WriteWayz down as grunts from the onlookers on the back wall signaled men were stating to stand upright again. At this moment, Cooper Murray again cleared his throat and got the attention of room.

"Oh yes," said one board member. "Cooper has asked that our next meeting take place at Fatty's Bar down the road."

"Second!"

"Our fastest second to date!" The lights flicked on and through adjustments, Archie was trying to help his dad to his feet.

"I don't need any more help right now, Archer. Let me sit."

Cooper Murray hustled by the pair to address the men packing their bags and folding the tables.

"Ahh, yes!" shouted the broad man in the glasses.

The room stopped.

"Well now … it has been brought to our attention that you have an unauthorized feline on the premises?"

"No. That was okayed my first day here. Murray signed off on it!"

"Good lord, Dad."

"No! This is over the line! Tell them, Murray!"

"Murray will tell you," a man said as he glanced to Murray, "that he doesn't have the authority to make that decision, Mr. Tapscott."

"I didn't sign up for this—any of this! False pretenses! False pretenses!"

"I signed for you, Dad."

"Oh, good for you, Archie!" He gathered the energy to rise. "I'm out of here."

"Well, the issue has already been taken care of, Mr. Tapscott."

Tapscott stopped his stoop midway between lifting his walker. He turned to face the congregation. "Taken care of?"

"Yes. The presence of an unauthorized, potentially violent, disease-carrying animal is, undoubtedly, evident to you, a significant cause for concern on this campus. We are in year three of a quarantine and another outbreak would be dangerous to us all. Well, mostly you and the residents."

"Mack never hurt a person. Maybe a rat or two, but he's an inside cat. Not some feral fleabag out rousing and rabbling about the streets!"

"He scratched my pants two days ago, fellas," Murray said, looking over a pair of new spectacles. "What if that broke skin? I'm not as sturdy as I used to be, and my immune system would've taken a nasty shock."

"His aggressive nature aside, not every resident is cat-friendly if you get my drift, Mr. Tapscott."

"So, where is he?"

"The cat and his belongings were taken to the corner of Tulip and Beaumont. He'll be happier out there, no doubt. Nobody wants to be living here."

"Second," Tapscott said under his breath.

"I'm glad y'all could take care of this. His whole house smelled like litter when we packed it up last week—"

"Archie!" cried Tapscott. "You insufferable sack of wine!" He used the last bit of bounce in his quad-Spalding carriage to propel himself toward his smirking son.

"Restrain him! Watch his walker!" The room began to break about in fits of excitement. "Call some muscle—an orderly! Not Marlon!"

"Dad!" Archie turned, finding cover behind the phalanx of orderlies rushing the scene.

Alton Tapscott saw the impending onslaught of healthcare professionals and fell short of reaching his first-born. He was out of breath and options—swaying like a boxer getting a standing eight-count. They approached with palpable caution, all the confidence of greenhorn lion tamers. He saw their fear and his heart pounded; his head felt like a spinning slurpie machine.

Laying down his aluminum machete, he waited for the uneasy embrace of an orderly.

"Enough of this silliness," a voice came from behind the folding tables, a man standing with his back against the window curtains. "It's a cat, Mr. Tapscott. You're eighty-two. Act like a man."

"Play a video game or something, geez. Watch the news. You like sports, don't you?"

"We need to see some significant changes. Let the record reflect what has been decided by the board today. Mr. Tapscott is to receive two counseling sessions until his anger is under control and next meeting is at Fatty's Bar and Grille."

"Please sign here, Mr. Tapscott."

The orderly, acting as bailiff, secured the piece of paper to his clipboard and paced toward Alton. Raising his hand not his head to accept the communion correction papers, Alton felt the breeze of the orderly brushing by.

"Thank you, everyone," Archie said as he grabbed a pen from his pocket.

Alton bowed his head and clenched his eyes. Whatever liquid was left in this dry, old man materialized in a single tear. Alton's scribbled name now held the weight of a wet diaper.

*****

He clunked into his apartment, dancing about and peeking under tables, calling for Mack. He checked under the dining table, where Mack hid during the prior week's hurricanes. He wasn't under the green monkey chair, under the bed, or in the shower—all the while, Tapscott called for an animal that refused summoning over the last seventeen years. He clattered to the kitchen, where Mack watched the birds from Mrs. Kirby's feeder.

Dust took shape around where his bowl once sat. Tapscott's tennis balls crunched through the bathroom, where his litter box once lay hidden. The room began to spin, and in a moment of panic and grief, Tapscott forgot his walker when he turned and fell onto the arm of his green monkey chair. Unable to regain his balance, he wobbled into the embrace of the green cloth, and sat, caddy-corner atop the chair, his shoulders and legs pressed against opposite arm rests.

Over the last seventeen years, from his retirement party to what he now assumed was the end, the orange cat was his greatest confidant. His wife dead, daughter on constant technology retreats, and Archie being a complete bore, the company of the cat a triumph. Mack never knew his parents—Tapscott had that on him. No degrees to compete with, or failed relationships. Mack never raised two ungrateful shits that ran off the moment they could afford.

They'd spent many a night together alone in the house. They walked among the oaks in the Garden District, climbed the staircase of the old state capital downtown. Greeted trick or treaters, hissed zealots off the porch. They sat in solitude, spent time in idle chatter. When the grocery delivery was late, they became firm friends over a tin of tuna. The two audited the neighbors' flower beds and inspected the sidewalks for natural erosion. They also ran flailing from the neighborhood dog pack.

When Tapscott returned from Mel's funeral, Mack was there to greet him amongst the soggy finger sandwiches, azaleas, and drug store digital greeting cards. He was real.

The green cloth of his chair sponged the tears weaving their way down his wrinkled face. Just two weeks before, he'd scolded the mailman for opening the door and Mack almost getting out. Now he was in the Baton Rouge streets without company or protection. According to the day's neighborhood watch drone report, a fox was spotted in the area. Mack was as good as dead.

A plump and happy house cat can't make it with some sly fox lurking about.

*****

He heard keys jingling outside. He tried signaling he was no longer accepting visitors at this hour by groaning toward the door, but people with keys don't usually wait for permission. A team of orderlies rushed in two-by-two and scanned the apartment.

"They already got him," Tapscott said, picking up his head for a brief moment in time.

They weren't here for the cat, he was told. The new medicine he was to be placed on would not sit well with alcohol. Because at his size, not many drinks were worth the effort at this point anyway.

E.B. entered during the ransacking, a large box under his left arm. He proposed an awkward apology, and Tapscott's face burned.

"Now, Mr. Tapscott, there's no reason to feel ashamed. See, I got a little fish I keep. Had to get it okay'd with the boss first though, Mr. Tapscott. Next time. Next time, you'll know."

Tapscott groaned.

The last orderly filed out the doorway and, in an apparent moment of personal reflection, he turned to the newest St. Ignatius resident and put a hand on his knee—his bad knee. "Don't fret Mr. Al-ton. It's just a cat. Get yourself a good dog instead!"

"Ugghhhh," Tapscott cried as he reached for both the burning sensation in his knee and his temples, his disposition that of a yellow jacket. The guttural eruption relieved what was becoming a steady rise in force of blood through blood vessel.

E.B. was unwrapping one end of the cardboard box, scratching at a piece of clear tape and biting it with the side of his mouth. "Now," he said pausing to pull the tape from his mouth, "this thing here is going to clean the apartment. The board isn't exactly happy with the shape of the room here." Slicing tape and glue with reckless abandon, splinters of packing tape shot through the air. "You've got some cat hair and some litter thrown about. We'll get it up. And, and you'll love this." His arm was in the box, fiddling with something. "You'll … love this thing. Newest one on campus and this one won't make a mess … it cleans it! Keeps ya company, too – God dammit!"

The box beeped, then booped. It sounded like a large fan started up, whirring as a buzzer rang out in short successions adding to the ruckus of confusion. The carboard shook and lurched backward. E.B. hovered over the top, hunched down like he was herding a bouquet of bubbles.

"Shit!" He finally latched on to the box's back flap and wrenched it open.

Like a snail from a starting block, the robot crept into view.

It was about an inch off the ground, hexagonal, and black. He'd seen one of these before, years ago in his house. Mel brought it home from the market after a local artisan knocked off half the price for the Texas accent. Of all the ways people communicated, an East Texas accent seemed the least pleasing. The company only made a few, and the Tapscotts only kept the thing for a few weeks. It gave its last "howdy" after running across some canine droppings in the living room. The excrement really hit the air conditioning that day. They followed the brown trail around the house and through the carpet until they found the machine weeping, stuck in the corner. This was back with the robots were round, which was more pleasing for the ankles, but meant dirty corners and walls for everyone.

"Hello. Mr. Tapscott. Would you like me to pair?" A woman's voice filled the room; this one Canadian-French. E.B. was snatching cellophane out of the air, explaining this robot was foreign.

LIZA buzzed in his ear, eager to connect. He stared down at the robot. This thing climbed stairs, speak English, Spanish, Portuguese, German, and Mandarin; swept, mopped, and vacuumed; and knew every quote from your favorite movie. It was arguably the most sophisticated piece of equipment the human mind conjured up in the last eighty-eight years—the internet and Nintendo 64 rounding out the list. The Living and Orifice Debris Disinfectorizor, the L.O.D.D., or Elodie, was a sort of welcoming gift from the great people at the State of Louisiana's Office of Aging and Invalid Services.

Tapscott barely made it to the toilet every morning. What happens when you can do anything, but you choose to search for cheese dip recipes instead? Well, Alton Tapscott made damn sure to find out throughout his adulthood. A worthwhile life defined.

"Pair."

CHAPTER 8

The sun peeked over the gulf the following morning at six. Residents awoke to the whirring of delivery drones and the slap of competing local newspapers. Somewhere around 2041, newspapers broke out of their primordial presses as people looked for a use for all the cut trees. National news was reserved for TV since the only source anyone would believe would have to be a video, and so papers spilled out with town gossip and the obituaries, which just came right out with the good stuff: "Mr. Gill Schroder died with $705, 201. 21 in his savings and his wife, Mrs. Schroder, is with another man at the time of printing. Follow up next week."

Along with the whirring and slapping, a constant *snip, snip, snip* floated about the air near the western wall of St. Ignatius Retirement Community. On the walking path side of the convent stood a three-foot-tall rose garden. Stretching for twenty yards this way and twenty-five yards north direction, the outer wall of the garden formed a square with a circular hedge maze inside. Each corner of the outer wall sat a small, saintly statue and a bench.

Gravel crunched underneath the flat, gum soles of the white size seven Keds that Thursday morning. The shoes fit snug around a pair of white tights underneath a light blue dress and habit, tucked behind her ears during the pruning process. With a snip, Sister Mary Clotilde strode on to the center of the maze with an intent pace, eyes darting over the flat tops of the foliage in search of twigs led astray by the evening wind.

Sister Mary Clotilde tended the rose garden each morning after her breakfast of dried oats and one banana.

In prayer, her small, thin frame gave her away as a vulnerable woman, but watch a round of her pruning in the morning, snipping like a urologist fresh out of residency.

*****

A slow rolling gargle of gravel invaded the area. Like a malfunctioning Panzer tank, the back wheels of Alton Tapscott's deluxe aluminum walker ground forward every few moments then slowed so their commander could shuffle in step.

"How the hell do I get over there to you?" he shouted.

A bird rummaged out of a nearby tree, causing him to jump. She didn't look up, but instead studied a row of pink flowers labeled by a sign above as "Gertrude Jekyll roses." Then her eyes must've caught a pair of splotchy, bright white shins, veined like the calves of a cyclist. His calves always were his best feature, Tapscott explained, and besides that, he would continue on at St. Ignatius as a comfortable man. "My wardrobe, my choice," he said, "and I'll wear shorts if I want to."

She showed him how the maze worked, and they walked along the garden path, Sister Mary Clotilde stopped to snip and pull as she went. There were nineteen small wooden doors that swung 180 degrees on the hinges and lock into place to create a new solution to the maze. Depending on which corner you wanted to sit yourself, there were over sixty-seven unique paths to take around the small labyrinth. Every so often, she'd stop at a door and peer over the bushes, as if she was lost on the path or in thought.

"We're lost, aren't we?" Tapscott said each time.

"We're never lost, Mr. Tapscott. But I will admit now that I am at a loss for your troublesome cat … situation."

"What else is new?"

Sister Mary Clotilde attempted to change the subject over an unhinged bed of deep red roses referred to in her *Garden of God's* monthly magazine as "Mister Lincolns."

"Mr. Lincoln is a vigorous, tall upright shrub, four to seven feet in height," she said. She voiced her aspirations for the maze to grow in height the farther you made it to the center. It would be a sight to behold outside of the community's brick walls—maybe she'd end up with a write-up in the newspaper. But the elder women of the convent told her to put away such prideful ambitions and focus on the tasks at hand, and to make the maze easier for Sister Mary Polycarp. If she got lost in the hedges one more time, she was likely to be placed at St. Ignatius herself, and the Order couldn't afford to lose many more of the good ones. Still, the Mr. Lincolns were an unruly lot, and she had to cut them from reaching their full potential.

"What kind of roses are these over here?" he asked, leaning down to look one in the bud. "Or are they all the same?"

"Are all roses the same?" she said, as if thinking that herself.

"They certainly look the same to me. Besides the color. Some red ones over here. Really red over there. Ah, redder!" A sort of confidence filled him.

"Very funny, Mr. Tapscott." She was smiling.

"I'm only passing the time. No hard feelings, Sister."

"These roses over here are headstrong. I can clip all morning long, but they have a will I don't quite understand." She bent over and pulled a long weed the size of a jump rope from the roots. "But they are part of our garden here."

"What makes a particular flower headstrong?"

"Usually its stock, or parents, used to create that particular hybrid. These are special roses in this garden. They can handle all the wind, rain, and sun thrown at them. However, what they can't handle," Sister Mary Clotilde stooped to one knee, "is the influence of a super spreader weed, like this one." She yanked and tugged at another slender vine that caused the rose bush to shake.

He never saw the point in gardening. "A lot of work for little pay off," he told her. "Like religion."

"Ah," Sister Mary Clotilde nodded her head, "a nihilist. How unique!"

"No, I'm not a nihilist, Sister. Just ..." he smiled, "just not convinced. I mean, I can be and have been convinced that most margaritas are good, and I'm passionate about that. It matters. But there's proof."

"Interesting point," she said. "Nihilist or not, if nothing matters but margaritas, couldn't you at least decide being nice matters?"

"Perhaps. It's amazing what you can still learn at my age, Sister. But I've always been a *nice* guy ... it's what landed me here, after all."

She stood for a second and looked him over. "It really is amazing what we can learn and make of our final years here. These roses keep teaching me. Better lessons than I get in the convent sometimes." She glanced over at Tapscott. She looked soft, with rounded features. Her eyebrows were plump and leaned over her eyes, causing them to wane into slivers when she smiled. Wrinkles crept from the corners of her eyes, the ends of which disappeared see underneath the blue habit. "I imagine it's similar to having kids," she said.

Tapscott shook his head. "Less back talk, I'd imagine."

"Oh, no. They talk back." She pressed on her right knee in a pained effort to pull herself up. She rolled back one sleeve and revealed a cartography scene of scrapes and bruising. "I said these were headstrong for a reason. You prune this branch today, and tomorrow you'll find a thorn in its place. They're smarter than you'd expect."

"Smarter than some of these walkie-talkies up here, I'd bet," he said, clicking his tongue.

She looked back at her plants. "I hate that phrase. *Walkie-*

talkie," she said with some petulant infusion. "Like that's a name badge. It's unkind. Just because you can't talk doesn't mean you can't think … like my flowers and your cat, right, Mr. Tap-scott?"

"My cat is smarter than some flowers. I raised him on the brain mix from the store, so he'd probably figure this maze out faster than us."

"Do you have any children, Mr. Tapscott? Humans?" His smile faded as the memory of Archie and the meeting hit him like these mutating thorns. "Were they unruly?"

"Oh, all kids are unreasonable. It's the disciplined ones you have to look out for, in my opinion." He told Sister Mary Clotilde about his children. Their mom was so strong during childbirth, then switched straight to the government formula feeding. Tapscott always wondered what Archer would've been like with straight breast milk.

They were the perfect set of babies, he went on. Both with their set of peccadillos and gave their parents enough of a headache to earn their stripes early but without running them off the reservation. "Archie was what you want in a little boy. Wild but agreeable when it counted. I think the most trouble he got in was smoking a little pot out of a vaporizer in high school, but nothing a Catholic school didn't accept money to go away, if you know what I mean." He told the nun about Archie calling he and Mel each Thursday from college. These check-ins became their last portal into his life as he continued his schooling at Tulane in New Orleans and the hurricanes picked up. "Then he met his now wife, and the Thursday calls turned into texts. Goes by Archer now in public, I'm hearing."

As for Evelyn, Tapscott talked about creeping his car onto the freeway on their way home from the hospital after she was born. She was in the tenth percentile in height and weight. A playlist was created to feed his daughter to, one that she deleted when she was twelve years old.

"I must have pushed her in the swing set at the park every Saturday for a year. Just two miles from here. The one with the dog park connected to it. She loved it, Sister."

Then he got into her teenage years. His reticent parenting techniques, and his wife's struggles to quell what was Evelyn's growing interest in holistic medicine. Evelyn went on a two-month technology retreat after her mother died, and Tapscott hadn't heard from her much since then, he said.

Sister Mary Clotilde pruned and nodded.

"Do you miss them?" she asked.

"The simplicity of children fades as they get older. I used to. But now I have, well, had, Mack. And my TV. They didn't visit me too often when I was down the street," what he was now calling his old home, "Well, not anymore." He was suddenly haunted by the realization that he was now Archie and Evelyn's only parent, and he wanted to comfort them. "The time that goes by in *here* is hard enough ... best to not think about if they'll stop by. Only Archie ever sends anything, and always through LIZA, and that's usually about some doctor's appointment he's set up."

"He sets these up for you often?"

"Well, yes." Tapscott reached for the imprint of Archie's hand on his shoulder. There Archie was, shaking hands with the board. Shaking hands with Murray. Groaning with the best of 'em when his father asked about Mack.

Tapscott shook out of his gaze. "He set up me living here, too! Without me knowing. No LIZA. No call then." The pair stood in a clearing now. He stared, captivated by the concrete eyes of a two-foot-tall St. Nicholas of Myra. "He stole my things. Took me here on false pretenses. False promises. That's all he's been to me for years now. Ever since Mel—" He let the thought drift into the past, hurried to his failing memory.

"But all kids grow up," she said, shaking her head. "They all move away. You have to let them go eventually. You can't dwell on what you can't control—"

"Everyone's always telling me this or that is or was going to happen eventually so why get upset, why show emotion, why *dwell*? I'll tell ya' why – because what else is there for me?" Tapscott shook his head, his chest rose below his chin with each breath, and he straightened his back. "I mean, if I can't get emotional every now and then, what's left? Jack shit. I'll be sitting around burping like some feckless bullfrog on one of these porches. Nothing left to do if I can't get a little hot under the proverbial collar every now and then. Archie says I don't get upset about normal stuff, calls it misdirected hostility, so does Dr. Addison. So, I get mad when a guy forgets to choke up with two strikes or when they're out of the orange muffins at Garden District Coffee but not when a nuclear war is declared? Drop it right on me, I say. I can't change that. I've got gumption for the first time in a long time. Had it at least. *Don't dwell*—it's a wonder anyone's upset at a funeral. I've been looking forward to looking back for too long. It's time dwelled on now."

"It sounds like your wife's death was hard on your family."

He sat still, marinating on his response in case Mel heard him from above or below. "She was holding the family together, but I can and have been taking care of myself. It's hard to imagine she was the one paying our bills, handling our cell phone upgrades … the big stuff. For years we'd sleep right next to each other, up until they put me on the sleep breathing machine, my arm under her head, her back up against me. She had a great ass, Sister. Life hasn't been the same since. I couldn't even pay a bill without her help before." He was looking down to his feet now, grinning out of the corner of his mouth. His ergonomic gray Velcro-strapped shoes needed a decent polishing. "She took care of all of us, but I think I managed okay. The kids were a wreck. But hey, to be a dysfunctional family, you have to have more than one person around, and they were gone. So ..."

"Who was doing that for you after she passed? Your kids weren't in touch?" she asked.

Tapscott couldn't find a response. Sister Mary Clotilde was busy snipping another unwieldy Mister Lincoln. The once tall, sturdy limb rising from the bush like thin scaffolding on a great tower, now reduced to a gaping, sappy wound. Porous as it was, but still time to grow anew.

"Mr. Tapscott? Are you okay?" Her voice seemed to slip into his ears and fill his head. It was warm.

He realized it was the first time anyone asked since his wife died, and he started to cry as his heart beat against his ribs and sternum.

"How the hell do I get out of here?" he mumbled low but distinctly. His face a sharp red, and his breathing quickened as he turned around three times to find his bearings amongst the rocks and bushes. They were deep in the maze now. He stepped forward, wobbling as if one leg was shorter than the other, and steadied himself on an outcast limb. Sister Mary Clotilde stood staring at his hand, her eyes soft and pitiful, looking at the blood run through his fingers.

CHAPTER 9

The days following Tapscott's meeting in the garden were a tedious, brief cocktail of check-ups and check-ins. Sister Mary Clotilde walked him to the nursing wing for an evaluation, unaware the blood thinners caused his excessive bleeding, not just the scratch.

The nursing wing was stark white with wide, hollow hallways. Only the sound of curtain rings flinging back and forth could be heard amidst the squeaking nurses' sneakers and rattling nurses' carts, that and the slow, repeating click of the call bell lights flickering outside of each door like a string of malfunctioning Christmas lights down the sterile hall. The dull tone of a phone off the hook invaded caught his ear's attention, then magnified as the staff laid him down, got an inch from his face, and asked if he smelled toast. He told them he lost the sensation during a previous pandemic. In reality, the stench of bleach and lemon slapped him across the face, singeing his nose hairs with each breath to the point he wondered if he really were having a stroke. He mentioned the date multiple times to prove his lucidity. He ran out of the nursing wing when they finished, fearful they'd ask for him to stay if he didn't appear bright.

On his way out, he saw a slight man in a large plastic gown. He felt the man's gaze and turned, but he wasn't sure if the man was looking at him or a spot on the wall, so he turned back as to not be rude. His mouth was open, a black hole stretched but loose, sucking in air with a grainy howl. Flakes of dry skin appeared around his lips while a steady drip of filmy drool trickled out of his bottom lip. His lean face sagged like wet paper across his jagged cheek and jaw bones, hiding his eyes, set back in the sockets like they might touch his brain. His face was distorted, and one eye—large and foggy—drifted slightly to the left as if untethered. Gums dull and yellow, no teeth. Tapscott shuffled forward and the man's eye remained fixed on him as if tracking Tapscott's heat. Tapscott noticed a nod, and his mind glimpsed this man a person--a real person, not whatever he was now. He imagined the man smiling, maybe even laughing--maybe he was funny. Maybe he had kids--or has them--and maybe he used to smile. Tapscott could see an old smile dripping with bourbon or steak juice, one that commanded a room and yelled for attention at parties. Or maybe he just yawned on the couch all day, his mouth stretching and contorting in practice for this existence--slowly stiffening over time into a perpetual pit. Or maybe he'd had a stroke.

The man began to scream, "Did they feed the cows?" in short bursts, like a car alarm in the night.

Tapscott backed away from the man's view and got caught by a woman sitting on a stiff-looking red couch. She tugged at his shirt like she was trying to tell him a secret, so he leaned down before she yelled, "What's with blowjobs and golf? Always blowjobs and golf!" Her hands were translucent like a skinned potato.

"I honestly don't understand either, ma'am," he shrieked as he knocked her hand away and fled into the dry, mid-morning heat.

"Did they feed the cows?" faded as the sliding glass doors shut behind him. His feet skipped across the ground, hurried by the sabotaging realization that getting old is disgusting, and he was almost there.

*****

He now passed the time by thumbing his apartment blinds and peering at his neighbor's bird clock. He'd yet to lay eyes on Noel since the death a few days earlier, but the man's growing garden and affinity for the aviary were evident. Mack would've loved the birds when he heard each tweet or the screeching of the TV, Tapscott imagined him jumping at the clock.

He periodically called on LIZA to check on Mack's whereabouts, hoping the old neighborhood chat group mentioned him. Useless. His collar had been found days before on a tree in an old neighbor's backyard. Tapscott stood in the fog of humidity most mornings, hoping to catch a glimpse of his friend bounding over the complex's cinderblock walls. He'd rattle some cat food in an old milk jug, hoping Mack would hear this desperate maraca wherever he must be hiding. Marlon swung by one morning and promised to look for the cat if Tapscott would just go inside—he was waking up the neighbors over the wall and a hurricane was coming, Marlon said. Looking out the window right before a big one, you can always see something you forgot to pick up or tie down—a patio chair or yard sign. It'll be quiet and still, except for birds chirping and scattering about; the squirrels have too much sense and are tucked away by that point. Tapscott hoped nobody was looking out their window at an orange tabby cat scrambling on a limb.

He learned Archie marked him a wander risk when the turquoise doctor came back to fit him for a white, rubber ankle bracelet. He could no longer leave the St. Ignatius grounds without the fire department showing up and a robotic dalmatian tracking him down. Tapscott tested the device's potency the same day by sticking his leg through a limp board in the property's southern fence—the rotting wood gave way to his sandal sole like a green memory foam pillow, and his ankle slipped through so that his toes touched the grass on the other side. There were no sirens, no great fuss, so he assumed this a potential escape route should things progress towards more honor board meetings. But when he made his way back to his apartment, the entire Baton Rouge Volunteer Fire Fighter brigade was waiting by his door, axes and spotlights in hand.

"Here he is, officers," Cooper said, scrambling to Tapscott's side, reaching out to touch his shoulders and elbows like he might spontaneously collapse. "Are you okay, Mr. Tapscott?"

"I'm fine, Cooper. I'm glad you boys made it, actually," Tapscott said, striding to the biggest one of the bunch. The man's navy blue shirt scarcely covered the lower half of his belly and had a faded white badge logo on the front pocket.

"They took my stuff and jammed it into this room then took my cat and my car, and now I can't even go on walks from the property, and I don't even know what they did with my house, and they steal in Bingo. My attorney Charles Logan thinks I have a good elder abuse claim on my hands—and I think they've thrown off my LIZA because I can't connect to my son anymore. Somethings up around here!"

The man in the navy shirt moved like he was in a body cast. His hips, stomach, neck, head, and eyes all faced the same direction as he turned to Tapscott with a sympathetic look.

"Hot damn," he said. "We hadda put my dad in a home like this, too, and I get it. Feels like you've lost sumptin'. I get it, Mr. Tap-scotch."

Tapscott shrunk into his walker.

"But look now, let's not go worryin' Mr. Murray and the admin around here by runnin' oft. These people care about you, and they can help you find your, ah, your cat," he said, hugging Tapscott at the shoulder. "And your car. Well, your car, it's probably best you aren't driving. Traffic is tough out there these days."

The man lumbered Tapscott back to his door. "Once they go, they go quick, in my experience," he said to Cooper. "One moment they're there, then they're … not there. Happened to my dad."

"Terrible," Cooper said. "Circle of life, I suppose, though. We'll keep an eye on Mr. Tapscott for y'all though. And I'm sure we'll get *the cat*." Tapscott had turned to see Cooper say this last part while winking to the big man.

Tapscott again resigned himself to pass the time.

The hexagonal robot kept decent company, knowledgeable without being pompous, kind instead of patronizing. Her tone was always right for the situation, and she knew when not to speak, which was a particular talent Tapscott missed in Mack. The Living and Orifice Debris Disinfectorizor's melodious purr was most enjoyable around nap time.

"You do know, Elodie," he began one morning, "well, what am I saying, of course you don't. You know so little." He felt Elodie sensing his movement on the cold kitchen tiles as she remotely flipped on the coffee pot. Tapscott stopped in his tracks and stared, knowing full well the robot knew his routine after a couple of days. Never the one to lose the upper hand, he persisted.

"You are a remarkably simple machine, Elodie. A good mensch, to be sure, but your wiring stops short of the simple things that make a great companion. I'm sorry to say it. I'm sorry as hell, but I don't think I can continue on conversing with a non-humanoid. Mack had a presence about him. A real judge of character, but your engineers didn't have the capabilities to add that in. Nope ... Nope ..." Tapscott said. "No, indeed."

He dribbled a splash of coffee into an empty, white ceramic mug. "And I don't imagine that your sociological or political ideas are getting any more progressive. Probably no political conscience whatsoever. Geez. It's sad what they are coming up with these days." He paused, reading the top of the mug that had "Happy Holidays, T-Pop!" in green and red font with a picture of him with a few kids on his lap. His grandkids, he imagined.

MayKenna and McJosh. He turned up his milk carton, watching the creamy white fill the bottom of the cup, overwhelming then churning into a mixture with the brown coffee.

Tapscott took to placing his coffee on the robot's surface and letting her take it into the living room while he fought his way through the kitchen. This was easier than his usual joust to the couch, coffee in one hand, spilling and burning, and walker bounding along in the other.

He released a prideful giggle each time Elodie slid the coffee to the ground at the foot of his green monkey chair. Such a simple machine, he mocked.

"The perverted state of our affairs at this home, as they have taken to calling it, are of most concern to me at this time, Elodie. At first, I thought I might have found a surrogate friend in Cone, but his meddling and political aspirations are not for me, I've come to decide. On my own, you see?" He glanced to Elodie for any response.

She docked.

"The rest of these people seem to be the usual vagrants, stupor-ridden old-timers, and excitable goofs that I'd see about the community college campus. This place is not the proper environment for a clean-living, chaste, and prudent man such as myself. But where do I find likeminded people? I've tried the internet …"

He grew up on computers. His first desktop dialed through the phone lines and took an hour to move the cursor. His keyboard classes in elementary school taught home row and dissuaded pecking. Never a pecker, but lacking the discipline for home row, he graduated to computer games, but only the ones his older brother enjoyed. He scorched through the America online years before settling into seven to eight core websites that he would frequent over the coming decades.

"That place has really fallen apart. Trolls and pirates. Drunk with power and a lack of sleep and empathy, red-eyed people run amuck. It's not a nice place. Not my cup of tea, Elodie."

He hovered his right hand over his chair's arm, as if to pet a ghost curled up in a faded sport in the green cloth.

"I suspect the nun I met with was trying to kill me. She lured me into a maze of thorns and boulders with no escape. A bitter, hateful, old woman—certainly up to something—and a sideways therapist. A desperate and sweaty performance on her part. She attempted to stir some melodrama inside of myself, but she has little knowledge of living with nothing, like I am now. She thought she'd find a brittle, impressionable boy, but I am neither, Elodie. Undoubtedly a right-wing conservative, she found my ideas on life a bit far-fetched—I probably scared her back to the convent. Sent her packing like a tourist without a souvenir." Alton Tapscott shrugged and crumpled his thick elbow into the chair to avoid touching the spot Mack indented.

"Yeah. I showed her, Elodie. I will say I was a bit worried coming out of that wretched maze. They shouldn't allow a death trap like that to be lurking on this campus. With some of these people? Liable to fall into the bushes trying to nibble a rose. I'll run it by Cooper—" He stopped himself again. "Or maybe I'll take some of this horrific coffee and pour it on top. Should probably kill the entire vine. Damn, Elodie. If you're going to make it for me, at least use less milk. Anyway, Elodie, I think I'll close my eyes now. You've been great company, but I can only carry a conversation with such low-brow sentience for so long. I've got nothing left for you and nothing left for me either, I suppose. I'll rest up and draw some strength, then they'll see me. Besides, they'll see how beautiful I am, and be ashamed. Archie. Archer. You'll meet him soon enough. Little twit. I raised him, did everything with him, and he takes off to New Orleans before I can get my teeth in the morning after his mom dies without so much as an adios.

"I wanted to name him Roger. You don't meet many Rogers anymore. He'd have been a different guy if his name was Roger. We scanned all of the baby name books when Evie was born. Sarah, Willow, Evelyn, Jennifer, Sally, Emily, Sara again but without the *h*, and Morgan. Melissa's name meant honeybee or brave, depending on your research. We picked Evelyn because it sounded nice. We scanned all of the baby name books when Archer was coming, too. Wallace was my grandmother's maiden name, on my dad's side, and Wally would be a great nickname. As a little brother, I always wanted to be an older brother, so Wally Cleaver stood out to me more than the Beaver. But I never actually met that grandmother, so it felt a hollow honor at best, and I never actually saw *Leave It to Beaver* because I'm not my parents' age. Oscar was my grandfather's first name, on my mom's side, and my wife's maternal grandfather's middle name. The alliteration might be a bit much, but I was teaching at an all-boys Catholic school at the time, and I couldn't imagine a kid introducing himself as *Oscar* with a straight face.

"Our parents thought this was all pretty silly. 'Just pick a name,' they'd say.

'But this will be his name for forever,' I'd say. 'He can't change it. Evelyn's last name might change, but his *probably* won't—unless, you know. This was just more permanent. Same first name, same middle, same last.' It wasn't, of course, but we'd convinced ourselves that the monochromatic still photo frame held by the Cancun magnet on the fridge was going to be some kind of strait-laced accountant. Maybe an attorney like I should've been. But he was definitely not going rogue and hyphenating his last name in thirty years, right? Hell, a friend of mine changed his son's name after a couple of months because their pharmacist couldn't pronounce it. Why they were bringing him to the pharmacist so often escapes me. *We aren't a dynasty or something*, my mother said one day. *Why do you need to name him after someone?*

"With four months to go, I heard a man on the radio describe how relieved he was when he impregnated his live-in girlfriend so his family line might continue. He was the last male in his family and coming to grips with lineage dying on his watch hit home as his son was born. 'I couldn't be the last one.' He named his son Jack if I recall correctly. That's a decent enough heir, I thought, but my boss' son's name was Jack, so how would that have looked at the Christmas party. That interview gave me a whole new sense of purpose with the name, and the feeling that Terry Gross might've been my middle school librarian. Also, Jack might be the best name a white kid can have: it's unique but not *too* unique, it doesn't have a silly nickname—it's already a nickname or sorts— and there's only one common spelling. Nothing silly like Casey or Kayce, Jeffrey and Geoffrey. But Jack Tapscott couldn't work. Sounds like he's got Tourette's or something.

"My name is registered with the State of Louisiana as Alton B. Tapscott, but the IRS knows me by Alton Tapscott, Alton Tap Scott, and the always charming, Scott Tap ... this should be easy enough. I have three different credit scores to this day, Elodie, and even I struggle with which is in the 700s. All of my past due debt goes directly to Scott Tap. Scott is living a careless life, in my mind. The IRS will get him one day, but he'll go down with a fight. With this in mind, I told Mel, I told her our son had to go by whatever was on the birth certificate. Well acquainted with the burden of the last name at this point, she'd agreed. She threw Henry into the mix with three months left. I said no, everyone was naming their son Henry then. She tried sticking to it. 'It's a good name,' she said. It was, but I couldn't have him being the next Cade. Before I was at the community college, I taught at an all-boys high school, and one year, I had exactly eleven versions of Cade in my classroom. There was a quiet Cade that became irate with me for spoiling the new superhero movie with an exam bonus question, a Kade that was smart but sandbagged his way into the regular English, and the Cade that I watched take his jacket off one blurry day and hand to an elderly priest. This last Cade would pass away a year later. One of the Cade's mom told me she'd never even heard of the name Cade when she named her Cade, Cade. She thought she'd made it up on the spot ... Caleb and Wade, she said. But no, I wouldn't allow him to be one of twelve on a school roster. He'd be an individual! I told Mel that Henry was the eleventh most used boy's name according to the previous year's census numbers. Mel's maiden name was Lee, but that was a bit out of style then for reasons a black robot like yourself might should understand ... well, maybe. We liked the name Tommy, but we had two nephews named Tommy. Melissa loved my middle name. I didn't.

"My mother's great aunt was Sam Houston's second wife. Sam Houston was the first and third president of Texas, so that's important enough for a virtual professor and marketing director's son, we thought. But we lived in Houston for three years and didn't like the sound of it. It reminded me of all the kids I grew up with named Dallas or Austin. And it was Sam Houston's second wife, so it seemed like a bad deal. My high school graduating and surrounding classes had a Dallas, Austin, Waco, Tyler, Cody, Cash, Rylan, JaCoby, Doyle, Vann, Silo, Cricket, Buck, Hunter, Farmer, Brittney, Brittany, Britnee, Jessie, Rhett, Donald Keith, John Kyle, and John Travis. No, my son wouldn't carry that torch.

Even the formal sounding friends like Sanford Whatley Gay II went by Bo, Beau later in life. Remington Browning Savage III was a class behind me in school. He sounded like a perfect debutant until you realized each one of them is a different gun brand. He got kicked out of school my senior year for having a Browning shotgun in his truck. What if my son named was Henry came up with something as mind numbing as the next assembly line? If it was a self-fulfilling prophecy I was after, I'd have named him Shaq.

"So maybe we weren't christening a prince, but we weren't naming him after a town in Texas. Mel didn't see what the big deal was. She grew up seventy-five miles from my hometown—a place with three hundred thousand. She had a David, Nick, Ben and Becca to my Cleat, Cheeseburger, Blaze, and Brynleigh. No, we could do better. We were better. I sat in the waiting room at the hospital just down the interstate from here in July of 2020. Mel was getting an epidural, which a religion teacher at the all-boys school said was against Christ's will, but I found the screaming from the non-medicated a bit much on our first visit. They asked me to leave the delivery room for a while. The waiting room had tinted, long windows that stretched from floor to ceiling. The tint didn't muffle the glare on the TV as I watched an episode of *Bar Rescue* on Spike. The show's hot-tempered host yelled at the blank face of a bar owner who had been drinking on the job and ignoring health code violations like his bartender peeing in the trough behind the bar … easy to miss things like that when you're in a managerial role, Elodie. When the episode went to commercial, the bar's neon sign slashed across the screen: Tapscott's. I was shocked. There was only one other person in the room, a man with thick, wide glasses on. He glanced to me, the TV, then back to his phone. I mumbled something to get his attention back to the TV until I could see I had him. He said something like, 'Oh, wow. That's a small world,' then looked back at his phone. There was this giant blue wreath on his knee, positioned so his dark jeans were poking through the middle. I asked how things were going, and he looked up again. 'Fine,' he said, 'just nervous.' I wanted to give some grand advice, but I was just in my thirties, so I didn't think it my place. I asked what the name was going to be to see if I'd gleam any relevance to our own search. He said something like, 'Oh, we aren't telling anyone until he's born.' Like it was this big secret or something. He said, 'We just aren't telling anyone. It's not a big deal.' I had to know, Elodie. I asked how they might pull off the name reveal … a banner, social media, or would a plane write it in the sky? Was this kid going to change the world? Why all this secrecy? You're right, I said, it isn't a big deal. Just tell me.

"He got up and left the room, and a few minutes later, I saw him down by the walking path encircling the man-made pond. A few ducks landed later, and I remembered my friend's dog died in New Orleans the week before … Goose. Goose was a good name, I thought. No nicknames, I thought. Just Goose. A nurse busted my concentration when she called me back to the delivery room. The delivery took all of four minutes—two pushes and two sets of heavy breathing and hand squeezing—and here he was. July 29th, 2020—my dad, and a niece and nephew's birthdays. I asked her about Dennis. My dad's name is Dennis David Tapscott, my older brother his junior, but he named his son Otis after the elevator. Dennis was 782nd most popular in the previous year's census numbers. The census lacked any evidence on Otis' numbers. Mel said no to Dennis, at least as a first name. She got Archer in her head from somewhere I don't know. I pulled out my phone and stared at the names surrounding it on the census ... maybe we overlooked something. Ezekiel, Ezra, Elijah, and Noah. We weren't that religious, and had we been, I had a friend named Noah and the letter E looks strange capitalized in a signature, so those were all out. 'We can call him Archie,' she said, smudging away sweat and tears, 'if you just can't do Archer for whatever reason.' It sounded like an old comic character to me, fiercely scrolling through my phone for an aberration of insight. 'No, not like the comic, Alton,' she said, wincing as the doctor threaded her birth canal back together. 'Maybe like Archie Manning. The baseball player or whatever.' I thought, okay, Archie Manning I can deal with. All right, Archer Dennis it is. We'll call him Archie. Or what about just A.D.? I proceeded to tell her about the serendipitous bar-centered TV show in the waiting room as she held Archie to her chest, his screaming lungs piercing the room and his little feet dancing against her stomach. The doctor rated the birth a ten out of ten and said it was the fastest she'd ever seen.

"A day later, baby in tow, I rolled them down to the hall to our car. She was crying, still gripping Archie, and thanking the nurses as we sped past a door with a huge blue wreath hanging outside. Kayden written in white string along the top and Cole in dark blue on the bottom—K.C. in the middle. I said, Jesus Christ, Mel. That's what he was stressing about?

"I wonder if Kayden Cole's dad is trapped in a place like this now?"

Tapscott threw his shoulders against the back of his chair, sending his legs flying toward the ceiling and the green and brown rests burst from the chair frame. His bare shins smashed the plastic and aluminum walker frame that he failed to move before unleashing the chair's recline potential. He winced and screamed, "Yow!" and his dry eyes clinched to hold in any moisture he might produce.

Elodie phoned an orthopedist.

*****

Samantha Cleary tried rousing him to meet for a pancake social one morning.

An orderly stopped by to take him to bingo. According to the detailed notes of the state-issued social worker he hadn't met, Tapscott enjoyed bingo. "Brought ya a sweet ride, Mr. Tap-scott," the orderly said through the doorframe. He had a new wheelchair. Onyx steel with rubber tires and an extended brake handle out to the side like a ladybug with a catawampus wing. Alton refused. His privacy was gone, but a ride in a wheelchair meant the last bastion of his independence infiltrated and burned. And besides, he knew the temptation of sitting in motion was too much for his unwaxed ears.

*****

One particular day, a week or so into his hibernation, he caught a neighbor staring into his window. A peculiar looking individual, with glasses as thick as he remembered seeing. The magnified eyes appeared like an owl peeking around the brick, every blink a violent clamp. The man was white, a bald head, and no facial hair. He wore suspenders that held his pants up near his chest. Because of this, his pant cuffs climbed past his ankles, his white cotton socks visible.

Tapscott retreated to his bedroom. When he snuck back to the window hours later, a crowd had formed by the center fountain. Camille Renatta, Poppy Burt, Nick Romero, Zach Majoria, Nick Romero, and Donald Rudolph, formed a crescent moon of wheelchairs, wander risks, and listeners. Poppy Burt's head twitched from side to side like a passing bird might listen in—glancing and turning enough for Tapscott to make out the silhouette of an assault rifle on the red backdrop of her shirt's sleeves. Cricket Kirby, flanked by Deacon Kirby who was holding onto her faded floral nightgown for either balance or restraint, held court standing near a bench.

"That old crow," Alton said. "Another call to prayer? The nuns are rushing the rosary again?"

Elodie finished sweeping and nuzzled into the corner near the front door and window.

"What a zealot. Pontificating on points and purpose of grandeur from a concrete pulpit I swear I saw an old lady piss herself on yesterday. A sermon near the fount!"

The robot gave no response. Tapscott huffed in pity.

He thought of Cooper. He'd love this scene. All the village idiots ready to make a splash. Alton hadn't let Cooper Murray come to mind since an hour before. A re-run of *The Real World: International Space Station* came on. Tapscott read all the O'Connor, Poe, Hugo, and Kafka he wanted, but none of them matched the product the crack team at XtremeTV put out in the 40s. Every character brought a little less to the table and seeing someone so low boosted almost anyone's spirits. "Mel loved this show."

The group turned to face Tapscott's door, peeking over one another like a mob of meerkats. He cut the lights and released the blinds. His back pressed on the door like he was expecting a metallic battering ram. The door vibrated behind him.

"Alton?" Another knock. "Hey, Alton. We know you're in there."

Another voice. "There really isn't anywhere else you could be."

The band began to sing with laughter. The scene in the

clubhouse on night one, then the scene at the honor board meeting, the sobbing the night after—he blamed Noel Cone for that. If Tapscott heard him watching TV every night, surely the neighbor caught his crying and had blabbed. Alton envisioned them snickering from their stoops.

"It's just a cat," they'd say.

After another knock, "Mr. Alton, if you don't feel like joining, that's fine. We'll bring you back an egg roll."

His brain sputtered to place the significance of an eggroll. He remembered a bulletin LIZA read to him a few days before. Was it a pancake social or Cinco de Mayo, surely? Days and nights meshed together like shopping carts at a supermarket. Unmemorable meals accompanied all breakfasts, lunches, suppers, dinners, and snacks. Italian night would be lasagna, but the cauliflower noodles, served for dietary purposes, were no use in jogging an elderly mind of simple, sweeter times. He waited for someone to visit, a family member or the grim reaper. You forget about time, locked away in a room in pursuit of nothing, time forgets about you.

Chinese New Year … *That is it.* Samantha Cleary stopped by earlier in the week to deliver an invitation, which the hexagonal robot woke up and devoured, and LIZA read.

Later in the day, Deacon Kirby would advise Tapscott to forget about all other holidays and focus on Chinese New Year. He told Tapscott that Ms. Cleary had an arduous row to hoe with this celebration. Mardi Gras was customary in this part of the country during this time, but Mardi Gras was tossed out years ago. Beads do not mix with wonky-walkers and hexagon-shaped robots. Besides, the celebrations mimicked Haitian cultural ceremonies. The Haitians didn't complain, but that didn't stop the Camille Renattas of the world from objecting. Saint Patrick's Day was next on the chopping block. The suffering of Irish immigrants throughout the nineteenth century was cause for much concern. Christmas marginalized free-thought with the inundation of cheer and good tidings—a person should be angry if they felt like it. Christmas was out. They tried celebrating Diwali for exactly one season. Ms. Burt found the ideals too reminiscent of Marxism and labeled it as inciting class-warfare and "definitely not Christian." Martin Luther King Day reigned supreme until Nick Romero read that MLK'd been to prison, and everyone agreed a prisoner was not to be celebrated. New Year celebrations were dumped because the residents felt midnight was too harsh an obligation. Chinese New Year made it this far. They all agreed that holidays are more enjoyable, the less you know about them and decided to avoid any information on the subject.

*****

Tapscott opened the door and joined the pack, shuffling across the lawn and sidewalks, clanging up the tin ramp to the rec center. Camille Renata nodded toward the Wander-Guard anklet, the outline of which stuck out like a goiter under Tapscott's white socks.

"I can respect that, man. Wearing shorts so everyone can see it. No shame. Man, I like that," Renata said, his face hidden under the shimmering green glow of the plastic poker visor with a St. Ignatius logo on the front, walking back to the front of the crowd.

Samantha Cleary was decorating the white rafters of the room in red and yellow streamers, "Happy New Year" firework images dangled from the crown molding edging the room. Bright paper lanterns hung wobbling from the ceiling fans and a dragon-themed cloth covered each table's plastic top. She'd recycled a few Cinco De Mayo decorations from the year before. Nobody seemed to notice that the red papier-mâché dragons on the buffet started out as red sombrero sporting burros.

In second grade, Alton Tapscott had used some carboard moving boxes to make his piece of the class dragon for the Chinese New Year parade. They'd dipped between classrooms, shouting "Ciao!" and "Hola!" to teachers and parents to the applause of digital cameras. The one Asian student's parents came to tell the class about life in China, but a steady diet of katana-less stories kept the attention-deficit-disorder prescriptions flowing. The ceremony culminated in a Kung Fu movie marathon and a carton of whole milk out of a small paper box made in China.

A local hibachi restaurant catered the affair with fried rice, fresh vegetables, and sautéed chicken, shrimp, and beef. Renatta told anyone that listened that hibachi originated in Japan, and Japan was not in China.

"You see, there's a difference in stir-frying, which is authentic Chinese, known as bào chǎo, and hibachi," Renatta said with a green pea and sliver of carrot sprouting from his teeth. All Minnesota grown. "See, Tapscott most Americans just don't pay attention to other countries like I do." He leaned back into the white folding chair, patting his small belly and pushing a third empty plate forward into the pile. "I bet you didn't know that."

"You bet I didn't know how to speak Mandarin?" Tapscott's fingers started the epic quest to the bridge of his nose. "No, I can't say I've had the chance to speak much Mandarin." Cooper was right about these people. Why'd he come? Was it the siren song of the egg roll? Was an egg roll conflict free? Why'd the robot been equipped with a door opening feature? His guts churned as he looked for the nearest handicap accessible getaway. "I honestly didn't think *Chinese* New Year was the preferred nomenclature at this point. Is it?"

"Well, Tap," Camille said, adjusting in his seat, "you see, part of the education I provide here is training in antiracism and in how to use your life to counter the significant and powerful forces that seek to uphold white supremacist patriarchal capitalism. It can be intense and disorienting to recognize that much of what you may've accepted as inoffensive or funny in your live so far is in fact a way of reinforcing hegemonic oppression. You will find lots of compassion for the difficulty of undergoing this process here if you approach this community with an open heart and mind. Be careful and mindful in your actions and words. We are accepting of all cultures here bu—"

"Sheesh!" Poppy Burt cut in. "You aren't allowed to say nuthin' any more I guess, huh, Tap-scott?"

Tapscott hesitated, measuring his response with a bomb squad's precision when a hand landed on his shoulder.

"Don't listen to him." It was Deacon Kirby. "He's what you might call a *Talkie-Talkie* … likes to hear himself talk almost as much as your buddy, Cooper Murray."

The table laughed through simultaneous bites and smiles; Camille shook his head in disappointment.

"Besides, this food was made with the jiàng bào method."

"You know, he spent two years converting the Chinese to Catholicism," Cricket Kirby whispered, her smile so great that her cheeks lifted her glasses off her nose.

"It was online," the deacon interjected with a knowing nod.

"The Chinese?" Camille said.

Tapscott blushed at the thought of his first days on the grounds with Cooper and E.B. These people had seemed pawns on the board at the time. Lemmings with rental homes. Renatta was a bit much on the senses, sure, and Poppy Burt had said her grandson was a Marine twice since sitting down. Face lit with reserved optimism, he felt a grin growing from the corner of his mouth.

"I don't know about friends," Tapscott replied as Deacon Kirby took a seat near the head of the folding table. "I just needed someone to show me around."

"He does it with all the new recruits," Zach Majoria said while studying a plump pork dumpling. "Poor Nick over here." He paused to stuff the dumpling in his mouth. "He," chomping, soy sauce swishing through his lips, "followed him around … like a puppy for weeks."

"Don't believe anything this fool tells you, Alton." Nick Romero was pouring a Pedialyte powdered drink mix into his unsweet tea. "I spent three days being badgered by Cooper Murray before my first honor board meeting, then I was set to pasture."

"You didn't go crawling back three weeks later during a resident council meeting, huh?" Majoria said, his eyebrows touching his hairline, a sneaking grin with a closed mouth.

"No, indeed," Romero spat back. "I just happen to of agreed with him that people shouldn't be holding hands on the walking paths. It's hard enough to walk around one person, and when there's two— Forget it. And it's uncomfortable."

The Kirbys stayed quiet.

"You didn't think it was uncomfortable later—"

"So, Alton," Romero cut in. "How was your honor board meeting exactly? Fun, I assume?"

The eyes of the table shifted from the bickering eaters. Poppy Burt asked if they said the pledge before the meeting, her face scrunching as if in pain at the news they hadn't. Nick Romero and Ian Wyble wondered if the whole board was there … had he seen Cooper's son? The captive audience hung on every word. He half expected some condolences or even shock. Maybe someone else would think weekly therapy with a nun was an outrage. But no. Each tidbit produced understanding nods or short-winded chuckles. There wasn't a surprised face except for his. The binocular-eyed man was listening in from the end of the table, thumping his suspenders a few times in apparent applause. His blinks made his lenses dance like a pair of strobe lights.

"That's what happened to all of us," Poppy Burt said, her winged bicep flapping as she rested her chin in her wrinkled hand. "He draws you in, gets your contract, then you're stuck! He's quite the salesman."

He would've made a fine politician, the table agreed, but nobody remembered how Cooper Murray made his living during his younger years.

"He'd tried politics. I think," Mr. Ian Wyble said, "but after the 2016 election, you needed some celebrity to hold any real office in the U.S. Then he tried his hand at real estate, I think. Baton Rouge was a small city at heart, surrounded by square mile after square mile of suburban sprawl, and I'm sure Cooper Murray knew just how to peddle those cookie-cutter dream homes."

"My sons in real estate," Tapscott said, almost as a reaction. He'd spent years telling anyone that would listen about his son the realtor and the big houses and offices he was selling and buying. "I wonder if that might be why he and Cooper got along so well?"

"Oh, probably," Cricket Kirby said. "Those agents can talk now."

"Our daughter used to be a realtor," the deacon said. "She just got so damn crazy about making a sale or impressing a client." Cricket Kirby shifted and shook her head, apparently from the word damn. "Time to buy is when there's blood in the streets, she'd always say during a hurricane."

Tapscott noticed Camille Renata thumbing the llama-dragon

hybrid pinata on the table. The layers of red paper flaked off his thumb like a deck of playing cards, and the hollow innards echoed when Renata thumped its carboard chest. He looked bored, Tapscott thought, and he looked young. He seemed fresh in the eyes or maybe his ears didn't sag quite like the others, but there was a certain buoyancy to him.

"Hey Camille," Tapscott said, leaning over the table enough that his stomach bobbed against the bottom of the table. "how did you get in here anyway?"

He thought the question was discrete enough, but Poppy Burt chimed in before Renata could shake the pinata from mind.

"Government is paying for his ass. Which means *we're* paying for him," she said, picking up bits of fried rice with her fingers. "French freeloader. Ran tail tucked to America for our healthcare and welfare. And probably the food, too." Some of the table laughed but Tapscott wouldn't dare rile Poppy Burt, their initial conversation still lingering in his head. "Don't you laugh, Majoria. You're adopted from somewhere and it aint Arizona."

"You done?" Camille Renata said. Ms. Burt shrugged. "I don't have any family in the country, and my landlord kicked me out. So, once I turned sixty-five a couple of years ago, it was either sign up for free meals and board games here or at a soup kitchen … and it's the same free meal everyone at this table is getting." He winked at Ms. Burt.

"What about you, Mr. Tapscott? Free meal or did you get tricked like Poppy?"

"I didn't get tricked," she blurted out, "I just was a little surprised, is all. They told me I was going to a salon appointment."

"We were headed to a Bingo game," the Kirbys said.

"I fell," Nick Romero said, eating an egg roll. "I fell in my bathroom, woke up in the hospital, and haven't seen the house since. Kids and ex sold it."

"My son, the realtor, told me if I just went on a tour, he'd stop badgering me. Now I can't get him to answer a phone call." Tapscott glanced around the table, everyone's eyes staring into the distance.

"Hey. Hey! Come on, now. Enough about this," Cricket Kirby said, straightening her back and nudging her husband. "Let's get to the fun stuff. Let me guess, Tapscott …you skipped mass, huh?" Cricket Kirby had her chin and brow up, looking down the table. "That's a no-no here. He got the nuns to call the meeting, I bet."

Tapscott released like a twisted garden hose. "Yeah, but he skipped mass, too! I was just with him, how was I to know mass was happening? Why wasn't he in the stocks next to me?"

The residents assured him that wasn't how this all worked. The binocular-eyed man clinched his eyes and shook his head.

Each of them was led astray somewhere along the line. Cooper knew the Kirbys wouldn't miss mass, so he told them walking off the garden path was permitted. They got two weeks of marriage counseling for disorderly and disrespectful behavior toward the grounds crew. Camille Renatta scheduled the honor board meeting himself after Cooper told him the orderlies didn't get overtime during the holidays. Got two weeks of anger management, labeled aggressive, and a behavioral hazard. Yes, Cooper Murray had gone after every one of them, almost everyone on the campus—except the Rudolphs.

"His goal is to label us all flight risks. If we can't be trusted in here, we can't be trusted on the outside," Ms. Kirby said.

Like a line of retired Rockettes, each resident at the table lifted their pants to reveal a small ankle bracelet. The Wander-Guard 780 came out in 2052. Its soft inside collar was supposed to make the wearer forget all about it, but it just made swelling feet and legs sweat that much more. The magnets inside of the bracelets kept surrounding gates locked and helped E.B. track the whereabouts of some of St. Ignatius' more mobile residents. Mr. Kirby explained how the retirement home business was a real estate and risk play. Keeping your residents in their rooms, paying a premium, was a good way to build a portfolio. A good way to keep the money you make was to avoid lawsuits, and a surefire lawsuit was a resident playing in traffic. They described having their memories questioned by the honor board, and each knight of the plastic folding table had, like Tapscott, succumbed to sheer confusion rather than memory loss.

The walls of the Rec Center were transforming into a jailhouse common room. The hurricane windows that seemed necessary a minute before now looked too thick and had an almost draconian prudence.

As the pant legs fell back to the ground, hiding the pulsing veins and purple skin, Poppy Burt's eyes grew.

*****

"Here comes the captain and Mr. Smee now," she cackled.

The double doors to the rec hall swung open. With the fresh air came E.B. and a pod of maintenance workers led by Mr. Murray. Today's embroidered belt had the Olympic rings on one side and gold medals in the middle. 2044 was stitched in red on the left side, "Tokyo" written underneath. His shirt color resembled a light red Easter egg that you dipped for three seconds, tucked in to his yellow, pleated pants.

He took a few steps in the room, scanning the decorations and buffet before proclaiming, "Happy Chinese New Year, everybody!"

Four of the maintenance men lined up on the far side of the

room, glancing about, heads and gaze low. The maintenance workers at St. Ignatius were pilfered from the local church years before. Sometime during the second Vietnam War, a group of political refugees went to the Catholic church for asylum. Some were placed in New York, some in Milwaukee, and some made the pilgrimage to Baton Rouge which had a thriving Vietnamese culture. The sub-tropic weather in south Louisiana resembled that of south Vietnam. After their arrival, police chiefs, doctors, and teachers were put to work as maintenance and housekeeping workers at St. Ignatius Retirement Community. They made a livable wage and were allowed free room and board once they reached a certain age and qualified for Medicaid.

"I know a lot of you don't know these guys standing to my right," Cooper Murray was now booming into a microphone, "and I know some of you don't even speak to them. Maybe you think you're better than they are? Well, you aren't!" he cried. "These are fantastic men and make this place run!" He was now holding one frightened man by the shoulder.

Tapscott was so struck with how gaunt and thin the boy was, he missed the next minute of the speech. A shallow chested kid might've been sixteen. A small, gray hat teetered on the top of his head, swallowing his ears.

"So today," Murray broke in, "on one of their national holidays, we are going to honor them with an applause as thank you for all their hard work. They do great work!" He began fumbling with papers as another group trickled in from the tennis court doors.

They walked with their arms down by their sides, heads tilted forward, their spines visible through the thin, gray uniforms like a fossil peeking through dirt.

"When I call your name, please step forward. Vu? Vu!"

The men looked at one another with amusement. With apprehension, the shortest one glanced up at Cooper and his microphone, took a step forward, then turned left and started walking toward the podium. The scene looked like a Pentecostal going for communion. Murray reached out to shake his hand as the short man attempted a bow. He then shot his hand out to grab Murray's as Murray pulled away to bow. It ended with the two holding each other's shoulders like a middle school slow dance, and it left the crowd buzzing with laughter.

"Okay. Okay," Murray said, red-faced. His head tilted in confusion. "That, um, did not go quite as planned. A *Communication Breakdown* for any of you Zeppelin fans. Any?" He paused again as E.B. giggled. "Moving on. Let's see, Pham? Pham!"

"Di ngay! Di ngay!" E.B. shouted at the men as one, looking twice as nervous as the first, scrambled forward.

"Well, look who's been taking some night classes!" Camille Renatta leaned forward and whispered to the table, his shoulders bouncing in step with his eyebrows.

"Hey!" Murray shouted in the microphone. "Hey now! If you can't stay quiet and respectful while we honor these men during a sacred holiday, we might need to schedule a conversation elsewhere."

The giggles died down as eyes danced across the quiet room.

"That's better. Now, next up."

Tapscott's line of sight opened when everyone sat at attention in Murray's direction. The crowd parted just enough to see E.B.'s glaring face. They didn't make eye contact, but from his seat, he saw a mammoth, rat-colored insect crawling up E.B.'s shirt sleeve. Tapscott tried and failed to reach for Mr. Majoria without letting this bug out of his sight. The dark, little body tap danced its way along the shirt's starched edges. It found footing on his shoulder and rested a second under the unbuttoned collar. E.B. sat admiring Cooper with such admiration that he didn't notice.

For a moment, Tapscott saw and heard nothing but the bug. Laser focused, like a pitcher staring down the strike zone. The small bug lurched out from under the collar and climbed up the edge, then, like a chameleon's tongue, shot up E.B.'s neck, over his jowls, and jumped directly into his ear, like it was sucked in the canal like air through a jet engine, and E.B.'s natural reaction was for his right hand, as if spring-loaded, to smack his ear hard enough for him to stumble backwards. He dug into his ear, teeth clenched and head shaking, as his fingers fought each other in line to the ear's crust. The red imprint of a strong slap appeared on his head and neck, his eyes watery and drunk with surprise.

Alton Tapscott gurgled in his seat until, rearing back in his plastic folding chair, he burst into laughter. He convulsed in chortling, his body a symphony of snorting and snickering. Tears formed and through blurry vision he saw the room staring at him. It was the type of laugh he usually reserved for a decent cartoon. His shirt buttons clung to their threads as his stomach expanded and he transitioned into hacking and wheezing, multiple inhalers landed on the table from other residents.

"I'm sorry," Tapscott said, wiping tears from flushed cheeks. "I do apologize. Oh, wow." He continued to giggle as he reminisced on the slap. Did no one else bear witness to the comedy event of the season?

"Mr. Tap-scott," came a roaring voice over the sound system.

Alton's face, burning a bright communist red, turned to face the speaker.

"Do you think these men's names are funny?"

Tapscott glanced around the room. Still with fear, his head

became dizzy, and he looked to the members of his table for assistance. Their eyes, except for Renatta's, held to the ground. Camille Renatta stared in half-amusement, half-bemusement, eyebrows stretched to the top of his hairline.

"Funny?" Tapscott said, in an attempt to sound confused but honest. "No! Not at all. I just—"

"You were laughing while I introduced Mister Do."

"What? No. I apologize, Mister Do. I was laughing at E.B., he was—"

Cooper Murray was steaming in front of the entire retirement home. "Let E.B. be. We cannot have such objectively juvenile, bona fide racist behavior in this community!" His face was as red as Tapscott's, his shirt and pants becoming less pressed with each moment. "I just ... I cannot believe this."

"There's no reason to cast a stone here, I wasn't—"

"Mr. And Mrs. Rudolph, I must apologize for this man," Murray blurted into the microphone.

The couple were eating their lunch.

Mrs. Rudolph raised her head from a plate of lo mein to mutter, "It's no problem. That boy hit himself aw-fully hard."

"See! She saw E.B. He slapped himself silly!" Tapscott pounced on any comrade would find.

"That's enough, Alton. Please," Cooper Murray said this with a real sense of pleading, like Cooper was looking out for him. He saw himself shaking hands with Murray and back in the clubhouse smoking e-cigars.

"These people have gone through so much," Murray continued. "They don't need some community college instructor making a mockery of their traditions."

"Their most sacred of traditions!" E.B. added, circling the table.

"Oh, let it go, you two!" groaned a man's voice from across

the room. "Find something else to worry about. He's just a kid."

Zach Majoria popped Tapscott's thigh with a plastic fork.

"Well look who made it out of his apartment," Murray bellowed into the microphone. "Was it a full moon last night, and it escaped me? What do we owe the pleasure of—"

"I came for an egg roll, not the pig's lips," the voice shot back. The sound was moving, but Tapscott wasn't sure if it was standing or sitting for how low it seemed to hang about the room. "Just kiddnya, Cooper. No need to call your son on me again." The figure slid through the room like a drugged Beluga whale, heads turning in unison like a tennis crowd.

"See ya, Samantha. I love the burros, by the way."

Samantha Cleary materialized to the rest of the room with her reply, "Thank you, Mr. Cone!"

"I hope everyone is having fun. We are, aren't we?" She scrambled in a straight-legged jog to Murray and wrestled the microphone away. "Okay! Thank you to our maintenance staff for stopping by and for all their hard work. Round of applause, please."

The table didn't wait for the applause to die before each head leaned to the middle. "Don't see that every day," Mrs. Kirby whispered.

"See what?" Tapscott said.

"Mr. Cone," Mr. Kirby answered. "Don't know his first name. What's his first name?"

"Nobody knows, Cliff. I'm not even sure Cone is his real name. Is it a real name?"

The table was in an uproar about syllables when Alton cleared his throat. "Who was that? I didn't get to see him."

The rest of the table sat back, testing the durability of their folding chair's maximum weight capacities.

"He's your neighbor, bimbo," said Nick Romero. "Have you

seen him?"

"Oh, I've met—"

"Very nice little show today everyone," Murray's voice rushed over the table. "But hell, don't see Noel every day."

"Is that his real name, Cooper? What's his first name?"

"It's Mr. Murray, Cliff!" E.B. spat.

"I'm not at liberty to discuss resident's personal information. If you want to make an inquiry, please see the front desk. In the meantime, Alton, I think we need another conversation down on the carpet. I will send E.B. once it's scheduled."

With that, Murray and E.B. moved from the table and toward the exit. The table watched as the pair stopped by the Rudolph's table and offered to take any trash to recycling. The Rudolphs couldn't be bothered and told them to skat. Murray got to the exit doors and turned back around to scan the room. He ran a hand through his hair before the doors opened and he turned out into the blazing sun.

"Don't worry, Alton," Deacon Kirby said. "You can redeem yourself next month."

"Next month?"

"Well, yeah. Today isn't Chinese New Year. It's March. We do this every week."

"She puts it on for the dementia residents from the nursing wing. They don't know the difference," someone said.

"You're getting old, Tappy! Might want to reserve you a room over there soon."

Plastic chairs skidding under the plastic table drowned out the group's laughter. Tapscott sat staring at his last egg roll surrounded by a mess of low sodium soy sauce and a small, white sponge he'd found in his miso soup.

Archie was not going to like this one bit. He'd once scolded his dad for calling an Asian man a bad driver. "He nearly ran over a child, Archer!" Doesn't matter, he was told. Can't say it. How would Archie react to his father laughing during a sacred holiday ceremony? Archie wouldn't understand, and Tapscott was doubting the honor board would have a funny bone to throw him.

He'd have to meet with two nuns now, he was sure. He sat still in the Rec Center as the maintenance crew began cleaning the debris around him, sweeping the shards of red confetti and rolling the banner back into the supply closet.

CHAPTER 10

Two mornings later, a stoic Alton Tapscott sat clinging to a rocking chair. The Honor Board was in the middle of a rebrand into the Elderly Ethics Committee, and Murray recruited multiple physicians from the area to come in and hear cases. Tapscott was caught off guard when the MDs didn't buy his bug slap defense story. It was disrespectful to cultures around the globe, and especially the staff at St. Ignatius—an adjustment was needed, they all agreed. Rather than expel him from the property, his responsible party, Archie, virtually signed permission to start his father on a new drug regime. A collection of solemn nods and whispers agreed—this seemed like dementia.

"Yes, Doctor," Murray had chimed in. "We've seen a steady decline in behavior and demeanor. Sad, really. Must be cognitive. Dementia, surely. Is there anything we can do? Therapy with the nurse isn't working."

Ingesting a pill was like buying a predictable lottery ticket. Some would make you happy for a short time, some gave the body rest, some did jack squat, and others strapped to the nearest surface and blasted you through space and time until you, achieving untold foresight into life's meaning, became the first living perpetual motion machine. Some, if you were lucky enough, could open you up to a class action lawsuit that might lead to hundreds of dollars.

They gave Tapscott the blast-off sort of pill.

An orderly came each morning to change his diaper, get him up, get him dressed, and get him out to the porch where he sat like a bug smashed on a speeding bumper down I-10. If he didn't hold onto this rocker tight, he didn't know where he might fly off to. They took his walker and gave him a wheelchair. It was a motorized black wheelchair with a sharp recline and a barber chair's headrest drilled to the top with Coke can tabs as washers. Green foam protruded from a large tear in the backrest, and the seat was worn into a shiny, rubber pad. The footrests extended to either side with black straps sticking out like whiskers.

Why? passed through his head from time to time. Why me? he asked. He'd done all right ... two kids, a wife. A vanilla existence but vanilla isn't so bad with some laughs sprinkled on top, he thought. He'd believed in God on and off, kept his head down on matters of national intrigue and important, and he'd never sought the emptiness of fame outside a couple of New Yorker cartoon submissions. I don't deserve this shit, he decided. His mind shot to the family trip to Disneyland—world was out of their budget, and Florida just wasn't acceptable to his system—and how happy he'd been. Evelyn begged him to go on those teacups again and again.

If only she could see me spinnin' now.

On the upside, he smiled more, and the piss was warm. His boxers were getting worn in the crotch anyway, so the diaper wasn't all that bad. Besides, who else gets changed and carried around? Kings. Not too bad for a community college professor with little to no money in town full of tasteless morons. If only the administrator that let him walk at P.C.C. saw him now. Tapscott's smile came across like a toddler on a roller coaster.

Poppy Burt snuck over for a few hours one afternoon. She talked all about her time on Facebook. A few of her friends were posting about their new lives in other areas of the country, which she admonished as sorry excuses for Louisiana citizens. "Sheep. Got another shot, they did. Sheep." She gestured to her shirt, a faded white crew neck with a frayed collar—the front had a large needle with blood dripping from the end, falling on crying children.

She told him about her work on the campaign trail back in the 2030s. She'd once spread a rumor that the senator she worked for hated all Palestinians. He didn't, she assured.

"Hell, he *was* Palestinian. That was the best part!"

Once, she said, she wrote a series of e-mails claiming to be the mother of the Jefferson Parish comptroller, and that he was using the money to pay off her student loan debts. Poppy didn't know the comptroller was a woman until they announced her dismissal a few days after. "Suckers," she said. "All of them scared suckers. We are all suckers--just looking to become scammers. Boy they've got us here, don't they?"

Tapscott thanked her for coming by gritting his teeth and tilting his head to the side. Sometimes there's no way to escape the truth except to live a fiction.

Before she left him sitting like a damp load of laundry, she told him she heard there was a new drug they were pushing. "Don't take it if you don't want your teeth to fall out and your DNA to turn into a billy goat's." She winked and snuck off around the brick.

Tapscott didn't know if the Elderly Ethics Committee leaned right or left, but he didn't care at this point. He rather respected Poppy, her conviction at least. All that work on the fake campaigns, ruining others' lives, and cultivating such a slanderous wardrobe of text-filled t-shirts and numbing imagery—life was about finding one's beach, a beer ad rang in the background of his mind. And besides, he'd told himself years ago when his mother had asked him if September 11th really was a government-funded operation after she'd been spending time on the internet in retirement, the belief in conspiracies isn't a sign of fading or absent mental capacity—just creative minds set to pasture. It was a creative outlet, he supposed, only slightly less troublesome than the proclivity to brew craft beers. Poppy was in stark contrast to all the rational women he'd known in his life—perfectly, wonderfully, deliciously insane.

He'd soiled himself five minutes into Poppy Burt's talk, but all it did was leave him messy and uncomfortable. He'd always been scared of republicans, not because they were Nazis, but because the threat of Nazism seemed just a celebrity endorsement away. Democrats also scared him, but he reasoned his tepid ambition might well suit a communist society, so he tolerated.

*****

A caravan of visitors came through over the next week. Archie drove up twice.

"This is nice. Weather is nice," Archie repeated. He asked a few questions before Alton's silence must has resonated. "Weather couldn't be better, really. Next hurricane not for another month they're saying."

Archie fidgeted with his watch. He shuffled out of view at one point. Archie then tried backing away until his dad couldn't see him, but he came back. Tapscott closed his eyes, attempting to relax, but it was hard to fall asleep when you're fighting extreme turbulence from the arm of your rocker.

"I don't know what you want me to say. They say, hitting rock bottom is not a weekend retreat. It's not a goddamn seminar, you have to create your own…" He shrugged and stammered. "I'm … I don't know … I'm sorry, Dad. I miss mom and now you, too.". "I-I don't know. Mr. Murray, Dr. Mengis, they said this is how this works. That you'll get used to it. We have to listen to the doctors, right? They're doctors, not us." He touched his dad's shoulders and moved his hands away like it might hurt one of them. "This is hard for me too, Dad. I just need a break sometimes, too. From the calls, you know? I'm sorry, Dad."

Tapscott was hanging onto the chair for dear life, like the emergency exit door just ripped open and the left engine blew the plane in two.

"Bye, Dad. I'll be back, and I'll bring the kids." Archie strode off toward the clubhouse, head down without looking back.

*****

Elodie kept cleaning until there was nothing left to clean. A rolling stone gathers no moss, but a stationary one makes a lot less mess, he thought. The robot followed Tapscott's every move now, docking when the orderly came in to put him in bed, waking with the first key jingle of the day.

Tapscott couldn't talk to Elodie since his LIZA was now in storage. So, the two stared. An orderly put two googly eyes on the top front of Elodie, which helped some of the loneliness. A noise, any burr or beep or stall helped remind remind him he wasn't alone, even if what's with him wasn't fully human. Elodie sat on the porch with him most of the afternoons, feasting on fallen paralyzed insects in her scanner's path. She tried sucking up a sturdy magnolia leaf that blew in one day and just about went up in flames. Marlon scooped her up, and Tapscott let out a great sigh when he brought her back a day later.

"Good as new, my guy," he shouted, taking a knee to make eye contact.

Cooper and E.B. came by a short time later. A wisp of a woman perched on Cooper Murray's arm, E.B. at the rear.

"So here is our main plaza. Sorry about the fountain, it's being worked on by the city's finest. Ms. Burt, good to see you!"

Tapscott heard the canvassing approach and mustered a line of drool in the name of protest. After waiting a minute or two, he began to spit what was left off his chin. It was then Murray called out a greeting.

The trio approached the concrete path to his apartment, and the woman recoiled at the spittle across his chest, his breakfast left a crumb trail down to his crotch. Eyebrows waving and bouncing to and fro like caterpillars in a frying pan.

"Mr. Tap-scott! Hello there! Yes, this is Fran Buchanan," Murray shouted.

All Tapscott could do was move an eyebrow farther up his scalp.

"She's looking to move in here." She was a slender woman with whisps of blonde hair falling from a tan, flat-brimmed summer hat. A sparkling purple broach that looked like a ribbon was pinned near her collarbone on a light blue jacket. Her stockings ran into a pair of polished white saddle shoes.

"Oh, he's harmless, Fran. I mean, Ms. Buchanan," came E.B. "He's not a walkie-talkie, barely hears a thing." He leaned in close and yelled, "Mr. Tapscott, we're going to check out your apartment to show Ms. Buchanan. He keeps a clean apartment, Ms. B., oh, but, dammit all, look what he's done to his door, Mr. Murray."

E.B. pointed to the lower corner of the door frame where it looked like someone took a miniature machete to the right side, just under the handle. The unmistakable sheen of aluminum shown through the cracks of the rusted hunter green door.

"Maybe it was his wheelchair?" E.B. leaned in close. "Maybe he can't control that thing. Too much power."

"It's not battery operated, E.B.," Cooper said, clinching his upper nose. "I'm sure it's Marlon or someone dragging him in. Something. I'll get him to paint over it, and it'll be as good as new!"

The tour went inside, leaving Tapscott to stare at the fern hanging over his front windowsill, rubbing against the door. The group reappeared four minutes later. "Mr. Tapscott, we'll have someone come by and get some of those old diapers. Sorry about that, buddy." Murray slapped him on the back.

"So, you see, Mr. Tapscott also had a pet for a time, but after his incident, the cat wasn't safe in his care."

"Oh no, a stroke?" she asked.

"We aren't quite sure. Medication adjustment, I'm sure. We have some of the finest doctors in the area, but, unfortunately, I'm not one of them, Fran, so I try not to speak on those matters. Let's just say he's not a burden and he's being well taken care of. Yeah," Murray sighed, "we'll have to move him over to the isolation unit soon, on the other side of the grounds."

"Oh," Fran Buchanan said, standing up straight. "I didn't realize there was a nursing home on the property—"

"Retirement, Ms. B," E.B. darted in. "More of a solitude kind of retreat than a nursing home."

"Besides, you'll move up to the front quarters soon after your arrival, I'm sure," Murray said.

"The board approves what Mr. Murray says, Ms. Buchanan," E.B. snuck in.

Murray nodded. "Thank you, E.B. Let's continue with Mr. and Mrs. Rudolph over here. They add a touch of color to our community and boy do they love to dance at the weekly band concerts!"

With that, Murray, E.B., and Ms. Fran Buchanan vanished around the corner.

*****

With each passing day, Tapscott succumbed to lustful comfort, more at peace with his new existence. Sitting down and watching the day pass from your front porch was a lot like sitting down and watching the day pass from an EZ-boy, he was resigned to admit. He thought about a time in Wyoming when Mel wanted to take the kids on a hike. He spent three hundred dollars a night for the cabin with a view of a brook and internet access. The grass smelled sweet, not like it did down here. Up there in Wyoming, it dried. You could walk barefoot on green grass without the soft ground squishing through your toes like Louisiana grass did then. Mel and the kids hiked up two mountains that week, slid down the world's longest slide, and met a real Native American while he sat and enjoyed the innards of the fully paid for log cabin.

What'd Evie or Archie do up on that mountain? he wondered. He surmised he must've missed the moment when Archie found inspiration to be a marketer, or advertiser, or adviser, or whatever he did. *Archie hadn't changed anything for anybody so much as a fart might*, he thought. *He's not so special.*

Then, to his realization, he found his eyes closed, clenched together like the next line of sight might be his last, and he missed his son.

He knew from experience, in both college and recent weeks, that the drug's hold would wear off in the next thirty minutes, then he'd be able to feel the crud on his skin and remember who he was. He'd stop smiling. "What do you have me on here?" he asked the doctor one morning in a state of elongated lucidity. "Morphine? Oxy-cotton? The old stuff?"

The doctor laughed. "No, the *old stuff* is out," Tapscott heard several cranks from the top of a bottle but it wouldn't open, "after Big Pharma lost a case. Sometime in the 20s, I think. False advertising or something." The doctor grunted, straining with the bottle between his knees and finally with a crack, it opened, and he tapped the top a few times. Pills rolled out onto his palm like purple hull peas.

"I never let a faulty product get in the way of solid advertising copy," Tapscott said, detecting a chortle from the doctor. "If you're trying to sedate me, Doc, I wish you'd just go ahead and do it. Give me something with some balls. No wear off."

"You want some balls, Mr. Tap ... Scott? I think I can handle that." He got an extra pill, the doctor said, to prepare him for daylight savings time.

Elodie bumped his chair that afternoon when he was halfway choking on a saltine and sounding like a buzzsaw through a steel pipe, and he swore she'd saved his life.

Maybe she can hear me think, he thought. His mind went blank. But he guessed she could've been running from the sound of his incessant hacking ... he wasn't the best company these days. He allowed some meandering thoughts to dance back into his head, nothing too sexual in case the robot was listening. Then, the sexual thoughts. After a failed attempt at arousal, he took a hard stare at the robot's edges, the little brush threads sticking out from underneath. It reminded him of some mixed dog hermaphrodite breed. Some change came upon him or the room. It was momentous, as if daylight dulled, temperature sat, and time stopped. The air was dense and filled his lungs without breathing. His senses blurred into the cloud of his porch, and looking down, he noticed some awful alterations to the robot—it turned first into a dog, white and scruffy from the ears down. Then into the wooden coat rack from his old office, a black stapler, a red-haired man named John B., a Toyota RAV4, and, finally, a little girl that Tapscott assumed was the essence of the robot.

Tiny, embroidered, yellow flowers grew like pockmarks around her light blue dress, her white socks pulled to her crisscrossed knees. Her hair was light brown with white ribbons tied around one lock on the side.

Always the liberal artist, he despised quantifiable numbers, their equations, solutions, and variables. Arabic, Roman, or the like. But now, he felt a tangible connection amongst the fog. They moved in his head, and he perceived his life before him. He was moving too fast but in control, like a downhill skier right before the wobbly knees set in. Then in his head, he began to confess to the robot, dog, coat rack, stapler, Toyota RAV4, small child.

"Listen, Elodie," his voice booming in his head, "when I die, which if the warning label on all those Pop-Tarts was right, could be any day now, but when I die, tell Archie I enjoyed it, huh?"

The girl sat still.

"When I consider my life, my undistinguished life, was that of an industrialized man in this nation only consisted of about twenty-five thousand days, and that about thirty to thirty-five percent of those were spent sleeping, that means about nine thousand of those days were spent in unconsciousness. That gives me about sixteen thousand waking days of real life, Elodie.

"Up to about age five or six, a first-world child spends his time waiting for the dozen years of minimum, legal insemination that will launch him into either secondary education or become a future gear in the labor force. In the event that he's born into impoverishment, this can also be a time of endless agitation and grief.

"Depending on his social surroundings, this individual may easily spend the next dozen years in school. Subtracting weekends and summer vacations, the industrialized man has about fifteen hundred waking-hour days of time within the most formative period of his life to pursue art, literature, music, and nature ... or perhaps instead: TV, Little League, Facebook, and delinquency. Whether he pursues secondary education, or enters directly into the labor force, the industrialized man's next half century is often spent as follows: Approximately eleven thousand days will be spent in trial to keep the wheels moving, punching the clock. While he may enter the cogs of the machine full of youthful exuberance, as time wears on, he will find himself spending more and more of those eleven thousand waking days doing what he has to do instead of what he would choose to do. He may be pressed into working weekends, further shortening those thirty-three hundred waking hour days which comprise 2/7th of eleven thousand. This two day a week dolor may entail such redundancies as mowing the grass, washing the car, driving the family to the local mall, or working on and maintaining his station in life so as not to offend the neighborhood by allowing his home to sink into dilapidation and squalor. His few remaining non-toiling hours will be typically spent in transportation to and from a job they feel no sense of duty, with perhaps an enervated hour or so of inebriation before unconsciousness overtakes him once again. Often his life drifts into mortgages, serfdom, and revolving credit indenture. Most of these activities are the result of the industrialized American man's attempts to assure his industrialized friends, that he is worth. If he becomes burdened with child, those remaining thirty-three hundred waking days are sharply curtailed. It is very likely that less than fifteen hundred of those thirty-three hundred waking hour days will actually constitute worthy life, and less still if he encumbers himself with that second truck, that lawnmower, or that swimming pool in the backyard which is now replete with leaves. By the time he has reached the age of retirement, his body may well be too worn out physically, mentally, and emotionally to spend those remaining seven hundred waking hours in pursuit of anything worthy. The average industrialized man with twenty-five thousand days on this planet, may easily secure only about forty-five hundred waking hour days of beneficial life. Perhaps twenty or twenty-five percent of his life if he is providential, but if a member of the working class and not the exalted, it maybe be even less. The middle class compels the illusion of opportunity, but after cars, college, and food, the right to get from here to there, to think, and to survive have wiped you out. Then you die an old fart like me."

He looked down and was back on his porch. The robot was back, attempting to reach a dead bug just out of reach under the wheel of his chair, bumping him back to reality. He took a deep breath.

"Tell Archie not to visit me anymore," he said. "I've been gone for years anyway."

*****

They sat him in front of the TV at nights, blasting the local news. Through the reports he thought he could hear a faint scratching at the door. It was a swishing sound that could either be the fern blowing in a storm's wind or Mack trying to get into the apartment. Tapscott couldn't find out.

*****

He woke the next morning to a soiled diaper, paralyzed arm, and a cinnamon roll. The orange icing he'd assumed weeks before was infused with some form of laxative because of his bowel's reaction and the unusually strong mint flavor. He ate it without hesitation, scarfing down the still-thawing middle section. An orderly came to change him, and Tapscott wondered how to best show gratitude. A sort of apology and thanks for seeing, cleaning, and changing his privates while he fought through Pavlovian erections

Andre, the orderly, scooped up the elder Tapscott like a snowball and lugged him into his wheelchair. He fell forward before Andre stuck out a hand to catch him. "Okay, okay, Mr. T. Ya good. Ya good. Sih-back."

And this time, unlike the days or weeks before, Tapscott felt himself responding to a command. His back stiffened; his eyes grew.

"Hey, you good. I gotchu. It's bath day, Mr. T. Let's ride, pahdnuh."

Alton and Andre went popping over the threshold of the apartment and out into the partial light of morning with a heavy fog looming overhead. Everyone was either asleep or in mass. He could no longer shower in his apartment, so he journeyed to the clubhouse every other day for a sponge soak in a whirlpool. Again, incontinence has its advantages.

The rubber wheels of the chair rolled over the threshold and onto the hard, white tile of the shower room. Another orderly was waiting, putting on blue gloves and a face shield which reflected the dull light coming through the opaque window on the side wall. Both Andre and the other aide squatted and snapped their hips forward, trying to lift his legs and back before he plunged into the whirlpool, arms held high. They'd strap him in and let him simmer for about half an hour before coming in to scrub him down. The warm water rose to his chest and the bubbles boiled his wrinkled skin. The suds popped at the top of the water line, almost tickling his chin. His large frame filled the tub until the water reached his collarbones. There's a certain romanticism to fat people, Tapscott once told a friend. A beer gut signifies a nasty habit but also a good time. For Alton Tapscott, his belly, arms, and legs were mostly bread and cheese. Still, he was beautiful floating in the water, ripples of skin and water spreading over his stomach.

"All right, Mr. T, you're all set. Hit the button if you need me, but don't let the button hit the water. You know the drill." Andre winked, pulled out a cell phone, and ambled through the doorway, the swinging door followed behind.

Leaving the whirlpool room while a resident was bathing was highly problematic, but so it was decided in the fall of 2037, privacy took power over safety, as it did on the interwebs and almost all matters. Tapscott forced his toes to wiggle. One by one. Andrew would turn him in in a heartbeat and the experimental staycation would become a nonrefundable one-way ticket off his rocker.

Sweat poured down his face. The burn of the bath helped release his muscles from their drunken stupor. He moved his toes, then ankles, then calves. His thighs twitched and his hands gripped the edges of the porcelain bath. He closed his eyes, fighting to slip his hand down and find the latch. His hand found the handle to the tub door, and he got the straps off his chest and abdomen. He clicked the door open, and it flung from its lock, the water rushed out to each corner of the room. Tapscott slid down, sprawling onto the ground like a falling baby giraffe. First his hips ejected like he'd been tried to the wave. He hit the unforgiving tile hard, missing the rubber mats thrown about the room. Water gushed over his bare body, seeping in the fat folds and wrinkled layers. Walking would be out of the question. Lifting would be difficult on a good day. He'd have to crawl.

Tapscott pressed himself to his knees, wincing when they scraped the tile grout. There were orderly uniforms and PPE in the supply closet. With any luck, he'd change into the white top and pants, and they had slippers waiting for him from the shower. He thought he'd look like an aging Shaolin monk.

He pushed his way across the tile, like a dog scratching its ass on the carpet. Through the door, he checked the vacant hallway. Still too early for anyone but orderlies and nuns. He managed to pull himself up against a handrail in the hallway and settled against the supply closet while his legs wobbled to life. The door swung open, dropping him back to the ground amidst a ball pit of dust bunnies, mops, and buckets. The garments were easily acquired, but he hadn't touched his toes in years, so reaching down to roll up a pant leg was more laborious than anticipated. And there on the shelf was his Simpson's aluminum walker. Unlike debilitating prescription drugs of the 2010s, 20s, 30s, 40s, and 50s, the efficacy of a walker increases with the dependency—it truly was a remarkable crutch.

"Come ..." He closed one eye and motioned toward the floor. The walker remained still. "Get ... down here!" he cried, this time with both arms like he was pulling in a rebound.

Tapscott lunged to his satchel strap dangling at the bottom of the tennis balls. He pulled and the red walker came toppling down, a sound loud enough to startle Ms. Fran Buchanan in the next room, her eyes red and wet.

"What goes on in this hell hole?" she whispered to her Joy for All kitten on the nightstand.

Checked his belongings, he found his wallet, passport, and LIZA. He never thought he'd be relieved to find LIZA at the bottom of a bag.

"LIZA," he whispered. "LIZA, hello? It's me."

"*Hello, Mister Tapscott. It is good to speak to you today. How may I be of assistance? The temperature outside is—*"

"Oh, LIZA! You're charged, yes. LIZA, call me a car. Confirm!

Confirm!"

"*Mister Tapscott, would you like to know the temperature today?*"

"No! LIZA, please, listen to me. I need you to call me a car. Confirm!" He strained his neck out of the closet door, holding the earpiece an inch away from his face so he might catch any commotion coming down the hallway.

"*You have thirty-three jokes of the day in your inbox. Read them?*"

"LIZA!"

"*Yes, Mister Tapscott. How may I assist you?*"

"Call me a car."

"*Mister Tapscott, you have been removed from all substantial ride share services in the area. At your request.*"

"Well ... what is a non-substantial ride share service in the area?"

"*Searching ... Searching ...*"

Water was running under the shower room door, creeping across the hallway. Most workdays ran from morning to mid-afternoon. Things were just too hot in the later afternoons, and he feared people would be out in the halls soon enough.

"*Found. Drummond's Driver School Ride Share—permit pending. Book?*"

"Yes. Confirm."

"*Destination?*"

He tried to remember his old address before realizing Mack would be long gone by now.

"*Destination, Mister Tapscott?*"

"LIZA, what is there to do? What is open? Where can I go? Please hurry ... I'm counting on you, LIZA, please ..."

"*There are two new movies at the theater—*"

"Theater is dead. Next."

"*The Garden Center at the Capitol has a rare strain of grass on display.*"

"Next. LIZA, please. Wait!" His back straightened with the idea of a non-pureed hot meal with real cheese. "Is Fudrucker's open?"

"*No. Fudrucker's franchise closed its doors in the spring of 2024 after three quarters reporting—*"

"Okay! Okay! Geez-us. Zippy's?"

"*I am sorry, Mister Tapscott. Drummond's Driver School Ride Share's pending permit prohibits pickups and drop-offs to any location with an alcohol license. There is a baseball game at 4:45 at Abner Stadium on South Stadium Thruway.*"

"Bingo! Book. Confirm!"

"*Buy tickets?*"

"Yes! Buy one. Outfield bleachers."

"*Drummond's Driver School Ride Share is waiting at the front entrance.*"

He slid into the hallway, a walkie-talkie again, hobbling back past the shower room flood and leaving a trail of wet tennis balls up the hall like a bleeding elephant trudging through snow. Andre would be back in six minutes. Mr. T hoped Andre didn't blame himself.

CHAPTER 11

A stone-gray cap squeezed the top of the hard ball of a head. Large ears and shaggy tufts of hair smashed out in all directions like butter from a mallet. Plump, smiling cheeks engulfed a bushy mustache. The bill of the cap sat atop two bountiful eyebrows, unkempt and wild. In the shadow under the cap, Abner Doubleday's stone-cold glare watched a small, white car pull up to the curb. The scrapes and scuffs along the car's exterior showed the wear and tear of an adolescent A.I. driving program.

In 2031, Hamilton Electric Motor Production bought out most American car companies. It was an American company, but that didn't stop Alton Tapscott and like-minded individuals from avoiding all Hamilton cars on account of their monopolizing the ever-thriving American auto industry. Hamilton Electric Motor Production was run by the Moon after they bought it from the Hamiltons for just 800 million dollars and a custom shotgun the patriarch of the Moons hand crafted in his waning years. Exactly how much the shotgun was worth comes down to how highly you cherish the second amendment. It could be said the Hamiltons cherished it a shit load.

The Moons had a son so intelligent that he dropped out of his university program to pursue a career in city planning. Most cities had been planned by this point, so no college degree was needed. On his fourth day, he noticed the traffic light system seemed to be malfunctioning due to solar overheating. He didn't climb up a ladder and change out the solar panels ... no, he made asphalt friction panels to place on the street which would convert pressure from passing cars' tires into sustainable energy. A city block's entire traffic and streetlight division would be charged for an entire week if just one car passed by. Get two cars to pass by, and you've got a party. Hell, you could walk across the intersection and power a small neon sign for a few minutes. Jaywalking was a thing of the past—now you were a civil servant.

Alton Tapscott had considered that too much local involvement at the time. The young Moon brought this technology to his parents' scooter motor company, which segued into their budding auto-motor division. The crack-team in the Hamilton Home Appliance Circulation Service (HHACS) used a kitchen appliance to trick a car motor into creating its own energy from the friction-contraption the Moon boy created. Nobody knows which appliance, but each car company had to sell to the Moons before it could find out when the patent dried up. One Japanese company apparently got close with a small can opener, but no dice. After the monopoly was established, the Moons sent out a press release with the secret ingredient in their motor soup. The message read: "A zoodler."

The automated driving programs came later, and then came the lawsuits. Alton Tapscott had always dreamt of finding a robotic car's blind spot one day, cashing in his chips with a quick call to his friend and associate, Charles Logan, but not on this day. This day he cursed the A.I. driver and from Drummond's Driver School Ride Share and sat white knuckled, strapped to the back seat. No sense in dying in a Hamilton car, but maybe a Volkswagen if he could find one.

*****

Decked out in the white orderly scrubs that squeezed his inner thighs into small ripples and sagged a little at the back, Tapscott emerged from the car outside Abner Field as the echo of the starting lineup rang out in the morning air. He strode over the curb with his walker scrubbing the brick sidewalk under a large archway with *"CHAMPIONS CIRCLE"* scrolled wrought iron lettering.

He dispersed a mob of school-aged children crowding near the entrance by pointing out an ice cream stand nearby. They scattered enough for the chaperones to chase a few as Tapscott slipped through and into the confines of the concrete stadium. Iron beams encircled the field, shooting into the sky with copper awnings hanging from them like cypress moss. As in an open-air airport terminal, the concourse of the stadium curled around the field, the walker clumped along. Tapscott kept his head down, looking for the outfield bleachers.

The outfield bleachers, he'd told his driver, were the last bastion of the common man. "Keep your twenty-dollar dugout seats and home plate view—if you're going to take in a game, might as well sit with the real fans. No padded cushions, no, no seat backs and waiters. Just a long, hard bench, hot to the touch. That's the way to watch a game." Tapscott repeated his father's preaching on bleacher seating. "'Sure, Alt,' he'd say. 'We could sit anywhere we wanted. We could sit behind third or first or home, well maybe not home, but you're gonna want to see a ballgame from the bleachers.'" Tapscott was pointing in different directions with his index fingers, smiling. "The bleachers bring together a unique mix of refuse and redemption, son. Civil servants and deviants banded together to bake and imbibe under the microscope of the sun. Only a dunce would sit on aluminum nowadays, but the bleachers fill faster than the seat backs under the awning. The beer and popcorn are hot and go down easy. And it's cheap." This as the newly licensed driver read his phone.

Tapscott climbed the dark, damp ramp toward the light and the noise of the game, and as he reached the precipice and looked out onto the panoramic of the field, the heat fell over him in a warm breath. His widened eyes saw the players running in, his nose smelled the burned popcorn kernels funneling through the ramp, and the P.A. announcer's voice blasted from the scoreboard speakers behind him.

"Get your fresh, meatless Roy Dog hot dogs at concourse 7C by the fifth inning, and you could win a seat upgrade for the remainder of the ball game, folks!" rang a voice from the P.A. system. *"Remember, when you're eatin' hot dogs, you want 'em hot, not dogs! Roy Dogs are the official sponsor of Louisiana University's baseball team. From everyone at Roy Dogs we say, 'Kick the dog and go Kingfish!' Limit four per customer."*

Taking the steps down the left field stands one foot at a time, careful to balance his weight on one side of his walker while the other drifted in mid-air, LIZA notified him he'd reached the row. He shuffled by, feet crunching the peanut shells and sunflower seeds carpeting the metal bleachers. He held his walker out front and knocked a few men in the head as he crammed his knees into the seat.

"Great day for a game, right, folks?" he muttered. He felt the rush of excitement a game as simple as baseball could unearth. He stared, befuddled by the Astro-Turf grass, and took a deep breath. The synthetic organ music played, vendor drones flew popcorn and gluten-free cracker jacks to outstretched arms.

I made it out, he said to himself. The feeling of freedom caught him like a stealing baserunner, and he wedged himself between two large children.

"Hey, batter! Hey, batter!" a man sitting a few rows behind shouted, spitting out potato chip crumbs with each gulch. If the batter missed, his enthusiasm rose with a quickened tempo and jovial spring in his cadence. If the batter got a hit, he blamed it on the pitcher. "Hey, come on pitcher! Makin' me look like a fool out here! Hey, batter, batter, batter!"

LIZA got him up to speed on the players, their bios, and the team's record. It appeared that the team was floundering as of late, but the new coach promised increased production from the corner infield and pitching rotation. Tapscott listened while one of the chubby kids threw an elbow into him for more room.

Tapscott made a pact with himself—he wouldn't worry about how or what his next move would be after the game, but, sometime around the third inning's mascot race, his mind wandered. He might catch a cab and find Evelyn's address somehow. Or, he perked up, since Archie was his custodian of the court now, maybe if he rented a hotel for a month or two, Archie would have to pay. His mind swam with room service and Pay-Per-View reality TV. Once, during a hurricane evacuation, he'd taken the family to a motel in Auburn, Alabama, and any *ref-u-geese* as the Alabama swine referred, got free pool access and half off drinks from the Christ's Conservative Continental Church-sponsored bar at the motel. Perhaps a trip to Auburn was in store.

All of a sudden, a crack of the bat shook the park alive, knocking Tapscott from his dream. The kids next to him grunted, holding onto his walker as they as they rose out of their seats. A quiet hum rose to a roar of anticipation, the crowd getting louder each millisecond. Everyone started to huddle, closing in, reaching out like bugs to a light.

"Is this the wave?" he shouted as he pinballed against the damp cloth of strangers' sweating bodies, what his dad surely meant by the bleachers being too fun not to try.

Then LIZA informed him that his delivery drone was overhead with his bottomless popcorn. He shouted his confirmation number as loud as possible, and one arm stretched, fought off the grasping child to his left. The black drone, whirring in midair, thrust forward like it was coughing and a big, white ball soared into view. The baseball hit the bottom of the drone-copter, clipping its spinning propeller and careened haphazardly into the bucket of buttery popcorn. The drone immediately released the bag, and Tapscott screamed as he lifted himself from the handle of his walker and sprang up to receive it over the throng of swarming hands.

He fell back to the aluminum bench. The heat from what little sun was poking out warmed the metal enough to singe Tapscott's thighs through the thin, white cloth. He'd been subconscious about the amount of sweat pooling on his back and bottom, but that feeling melted with excitement of the moment. Popcorn spilled over the edge of the red and white paper bag. He fought the urge to gobble up the hot yellow puffs, but still managed to lean in with his mouth and scoop up a few kernels while his hands scrambled about the bucket in search of the ball. His fingers ran over the dull outer shell, and he held tight. Dusting off the ash of burnt kernels and rubbing streaks of butter from the soft, white cowhide, he gazed at the serpentine red lacing and found the dent where the batter smacked this one. His eyes grew.

"Ya know," a portly woman in a purple sequined shirt said, standing on the row in front, her hair—blonde and black—sat matted to a soft forehead through pebbles of perspiration, "that was my boy's ball. It was goin' right at 'im."

The crowd booed and hissed as a player jogging the bases danced around the third bag. Tapscott sat in stunned silence. He caught a home run ball. He'd attended games for decades, half a century at this point. Big league ballparks, Little League, high school, college, and the minors, and until now he'd never gotten close to catching anything. Sure, he got thrown a ball by Rusty Greer in Dallas one time, but that was just because he was the only kid in a Rusty Greer jersey. They were out of the Juan

Gonzalez and the Jose Conseco, so his dad feigned the high ground and made him settle for the one guy that might not be on steroids.

*****

"Hey, buddy! Hey, buddy!"

Tapscott shook from his stupor. The mob around him glared. "Um, yes? Do you see what I just did?!" He stuck out the ball to the crowd of what he assumed were non-believers. "This old man's got a few tricks up his sleeve after all, I guess!" He scanned the faces for a smile but came up empty.

"Hey, buddy!"

"Yes, sir! You, sir ... what is it you need?" "That's the other team's homer."

"Or my son's ball," chimed in the large woman, still shading the row from the front. "Or you rootin' for them?"

"So, what of it? I'm wearing my summer whites today," Tapscott said, pulling the ball in to his chest. "I'm a neutral observer."

"Oh, so ain't a Kingfish fan, huh?"

"A fan?" Tapscott said. "No. Not of this iteration. An alum though, yes."

"What's goin' on with that red walker, huh? Not the school colors."

"A graduate, huh?" a man shouted from behind.

"Smart, huh?" the chubby kid in dark purple jersey standing next to the large woman said.

"I don't think you quite understand the declining state of the educational system in this state, son." Tapscott started smiling. "But I never let my education here get in the way of my schoolin'. That's Twain for ya."

"Two-ain?" the boy asked, contorting his face up to his mom.

"Stop tryna teach mah sun—that's mah right, not yours, and give me that ball!" the woman shrieked.

"Hey, buddy." The crowd parted, and a man emerged in frayed jean shorts, a camo hat atop his head. "I don't give a good damn about the kid, but if you're gonna sit out here, you're gonna throw that ball back on that field where it belongs." He gestured toward the baseball diamond with a rough, gnarled nub of an index finger. Standing straight up, his shadow almost reaching Mr. Tapscott's shower shoes from a short distance away. "And do it with some gusto."

Tapscott saw the man's brow lumping over his eyes, which were a pair of black dots looking him up and down.

"Say, what is it you're wearing?"

Tapscott sat still, remembering the breeze and the attention washing over his body from his bare ankles up to the white paper band taped around his wrist.

"You with the government, buddy?"

"The government?"

"Yeah. What's that band?"

"Looks like he was in the hospital," a voice called.

"With the vi-rus?" a small, blond boy with a red face asked his mom, tugging on her blouse.

"Why would you think that? The virus? Heavens no." Tapscott reconsidered. "Well, maybe I do have a virus? Can you really tell these days? You'd best back away! It's probably highly contagious."

A soft buzz picked up as the crowd backed away, and Tapscott felt a tug from behind, hard enough on his thin shirt that it might rip. He turned to find the other kid, his fat, swollen fingers motioning for Alton to bend down. With his eyebrows and eyes wide and a pleasant tone and smile, as he felt customary when dealing with feral children, he asked the boy, "Can I help you, sir?"

"I'm not scared of no vi-rus. I've had the chicken pox and was fine. I want that ball," he said, holding out an empty, black baseball glove.

Alton glanced around. He remembered his father. These people were desecrating the polished name of bleacher sitting. The audacity of this kid's request. He remembered Mack ... who'd have avoided Alton for a week if he'd ever gone to such lengths to work up a sweat like he had going now.

"Well, son," he said, leaning down a bit farther until the sour stench of mustard on the kid's shirt reached his nose, "you ain't getting shit."

*****

"Get 'im!"

The crowd erupted: popcorn flew, the boy's momma began waving her clear handbag like a mace above Alton Tapscott as the rest of the onlookers swarmed him, scratching and clawing his right hand, while his left clamped onto his Simpson's walker. Tapscott felt a bite on his thigh, so he bit back at a hairy, sweaty arm. He heard himself growl. A woman screamed that someone rolled over her nachos. He landed a hard left heel into something that cracked.

He fell back on the metal of the stadium steps, and his shower shoes slipped off as his wet feet danced in the air, kicking like a mule. Two firm hands grasped his bare ankles, and in a quick swoop, he went skidding out from the swirling crowd, his shirt coming up behind him, scraping his back on the peanuts and coarse bleacher bottom.

He grit his teeth while grabbing his back, the searing strips of skinless hide already producing some pointillist blood pattern.

"Get 'im outta here!" the crowd shouted as a man in a navy-blue track suit lifted Tapscott to his feet. The man gripped Tapscott's shoulder, and with only a thumb pressed on his neck propelled him forward.

"I got the ball!" Tapscott shouted back. "I still got it! You jackals! Little greedy curs!"

The man bent Tapscott's arm around behind him, shoveling him up the stairs toward the dark tunnel.

The speakers around the stadium played a man yelling "*You'rrrre OUTTA here!*" as Tapscott glanced up to see the back of his sweaty, gleaming head disappearing into the tunnel from the jumbotron. A chorus of cheers chased after him then faded as they entered the concourse; his eye adjusted to see Marlon in his bright teal blue scrubs.

CHAPTER 12

Alton Tapscott, with a matted, messy head of hair, emerged from his apartment at the St. Ignatius Retirement Home that evening dressed for battle. His fresh, white robe, the static still audibly present, brown leather sandals strapped so they carved into the veins on the tops of his feet, and jewelry—a white bracelet monitor dangling from his right ankle. The orderly offered him a wheelchair, but he turned it down. He walked out into the orange glow of the fading day, forgetting all about the red walker propped up against the front window.

Noel Cone, Camille Renata, Zach Majoria, Nick Romero, the Kirbys, the Rows, and Poppy Burt congregated around the fountain and nodded as Mr. Tapscott strode by a few paces ahead of the orderly. The Wybles and the Richards paused their Mahjong game in the next courtyard, their heads shaking with sorrowful expressions.

"We'll be seein' ya, Tappy." One of them crooked his head away from the table and nodded.

$$*****$$

The room had a kind of twenty-four-hour diner ambiance. The maple syrup hit his nostrils as he entered, the lull of fluorescent lighting, and the vague feeling that everything he touched would be sticky. Tapscott stood in the doorway, his stance wide and wobbling like an asthmatic outlaw.

He entered and scanned the room to find members of the Elderly Ethics Committee in the corner, all standing with their backs to the room, pointing out a window. There Archie was in the opposite corner, looking down at his phone with as sure a grimace as his dad had seen in years. A man and a woman stood in the middle of the room. The man he recognized as the facility's director, was pointing at some light fixtures in the ceiling while the woman, in a small, gray suit, scribbled on a stark white electronic pad.

"Just get it fixed," she was saying with a piercing twang in her voice that made the word *fixed* have three syllables.

The director went about assuring her a call had been made but that it was being taken care of, and he waved his hand as Marlon came forward with a wooden stepladder.

The air was hot, and Tapscott knew his knees wouldn't stand forever. Try as he might, the walker was prescribed for a reason, and he wouldn't ask the orderly to run back for it.

"Mr. Tapscotch ... hello, hello. Good to see you again." The director ran forward, a hand outstretched for Alton to take.

"Good to meet you, sir," Tapscott said. "I've seen you around a little—"

"Meet? No, no. We've met plenty, Mr. Tapscotch." He threw his arm around Alton, which almost caused him to flop to the floor before the woman in gray stepped into view. "He gets confused. We provide some of the best memory care you can find but the trick is getting them to remember to go to it."

Alton felt the heat coming through the man's shirt.

"This is Mr. Taps-Cott?" she asked the director with a slow, deliberate pace as though her mouth was catching up to where her brain had been waiting. She opened a large, leather bag and pulled out an array of papers that thumped in her hand. "It says on his charr he uses wall-king assistance. Where's 'is charr?"

Tapscott and the director stood in silence, Tapscott glancing back and forth between the two. He'd seen some good country people before, and he looked at her hands. His dad had always told him you could judge a man by how soft his hands were, and her hands were twice as rough as Alton's, he imagined. The voice trailed in his head, bouncing between each ear.

"You must be with the state," he said, looking to the director for some guidance.

The director had a finger stretched in front of him, paused in thought. "Oh, so his *chart* says he needs walking assistance and you're looking for his *chair*. That's right, isn't it?" The director laughed like he'd just solved a Rubik's cube by kicking it. "Well, sometimes our residents actually see such an uptick in activity on our campus that they don't require physical or cognitive assistance anymore. We are all about healing here, Ms. Ledbetter."

A cold expression on her face. A cocktail of stark, mild features—her hairline was straight across with a puff of bouffant bangs pulled back to her scalp and a tight, tiny wad of hair in a ball at the top of her head. Her eyebrows were sharp but not noticeable, and her eyes a muddled gray. Her lips were so pale and small, that when she closed her mouth, it looked like her chin doubled in size. Tapscott guessed she probably didn't weigh enough to set off a car's passenger seatbelt alarm, and he was frightened.

"If he doesn't have his wall-king assistance, he needs a note from the medical director. This is the second time I've asked for the medical director to come up today." She widened her eyes and repeated herself, "I would go call him." She nodded at the director.

He was off through the door as Tapscott heard a commotion of tables and chairs screeching to the center of the room.

*****

The emergency meeting of the Elderly Ethics Committee was called to order. Two of the six board members couldn't make it—one was fishing and the other was taking care of some personal matter that caused the other members to stifle a laugh. They announced that Gunnar, Murray's son, would fill in this time alongside his dad.

Gunnar was tall and sturdy, built like a bomb shelter with a wide, athletic frame. A starched blue shirt with pearl buttons climbing all the way to his throat and an Adam's apple pouring out over the collar like a gob of gruyere over a bowl of French onion soup. His thick jawline made his bare chin noticeable, and his forehead gleamed in the muted glow of the overhead lighting – his hair was pulled back enough that Alton assumed it was tied, and Gunnar's temples were either straining or naturally tense. Murray sat at Gunnar's left, leaning forward on his elbow.

Tapscott sat in the middle of the room in the same winged-back, satin armchair he endured the first meeting.

"So," a figure at the far end of the folding table said, "here we are *again*, I guess."

"Got us all up here, *again*, worried about you, Dad," Archie said.

Alton didn't turn to see him at the back of the room.

Another figure at the table leaned forward, this one a smaller man in a faded green plaid shirt and thick-framed glasses pushed down his nose. "It's just frustration at this point. We're all trying except you, it seems," he said.

Alton felt his face turning red. He'd been trying like hell.

"Look what you did to your back today, Mr. Tapscott. We have to look out for you if you can't look out for yourself."

"And you clearly cannot look after yourself."

"And to sully the name of the St. Ignatius community while you're at it. You were on TV today ... a grown man fighting for a baseball! It's not what we're about here."

Tapscott didn't know he'd made the news. He was cooking up a response to each hurling question when this tidbit broke his concentration.

Was I on the news or in the news? he wondered. *Print media is dead*, he reminded himself. Nobody would read about it with all the pop-up ads on the local paper's failing website. Well, they said TV, so he must've been on the noon news bulletin. Why didn't LIZA tell him? He napped all afternoon after the pain medication for his scabbing back took hold, so the whole day must've flown right by. If Mel could see him now.

"Are you listening, Mr. Alton? Tapscott?" Cooper Murray interrupted the committee. "Sometimes he zones out. I've witnessed more times than not lately."

"He's been doing that for years," Archie said from the back. "But Mr. Murray is right. More times than not lately."

"You've embarrassed us today, Mr. Tapscott. And all while we're attempting to be a pillar in the community."

"Why are you doing this right now, Dad?" Archie asked. "Mom would be really embarrassed. You know that, right?"

Of course, she'd be embarrassed by this, but she wasn't here, and this is how he was going out. *That's the tragedy of this generation*, he said to himself, *they've got no style. Why go out quietly when you can huff a hot tailpipe and get your name in the paper?*

They reviewed his medicine, and all agreed it was accomplishing its prescribed effect. "Passive liveliness," they added.

"A certain degree of apathy isn't the worst thing for a man with his blood pressure," posited a man on the left side with an accent that left Alton wondering which area of Mississippi he must've crawled in from.

They really brought in the cavalry ... a Mississippian on an honor panel. He shivered at the thought.

Then they brought in a host of witnesses, none of whom described the scene at the ballpark except Marlon, who only caught the extraction, so Tapscott was still left without a full description of his great catch—his most public triumph to date. The L.O.D.D. came atop a rattling food cart, unveiled by E.B. like it was a baked Alaska. Before too long, the committee realized the robot didn't speak but could transmit recorded audio. Tapscott heard his voice coming from the machine, a bit too shrill for his liking, carrying on about the state of local politics before forsaking Mack's listening abilities compared to the robot's.

"Elodie," his voice said, "I'm afraid I'll never be able to fully comprehend the role of a Parish comptroller." Then the distinct sound of unzipping pants and urine splatter rushed the committee to excuse the robot, and an orderly rolled the cart back into the hall.

Poppy Burt came in to ask if anyone knew if Tapscott got the flu shot that year and that was clouding his mind, but she was ushered out faster than the robot and nun.

Sister Mary Clotilde came for a brief moment, her white cloth shoes gliding across the green den carpet, stopping to pray over Alton before announcing her professional diagnosis: loneliness. And an instinctive hostility to any form of devotion outside of his cat, she added. They asked how she evaluated him, and she announced the question she asks all of the residents during a behavioral modification session: if you had one superpower, would it be invisibility or flight?

The group of men laughed then asked what he'd picked, and she said he declined, choosing to change the temperature of any room he walked into instead.

E.B. brought the snipped ankle monitor to the table to pass around. They agreed someone of Alton's age shouldn't be handling an object sharp enough to cut that off.

"I think there's one thing left to do," Gunnar Murray said. "And are we all in agreement?"

The committee nodded.

"We have to find you a locked unit, Mr. Tapscott. For your safety, and for the community. Someone could've gotten hurt today."

Tapscott was lost in thought and embarrassment, like someone that's been pitied. A locked unit would mean no more outdoors, which he didn't mind at the moment, but there were other drawbacks he was sure—the man with the cows, and the woman with the golf and blowjobs.

"Technically someone did get hurt. A boy is suing for intentional infliction of emotional distress."

"Oh, I know someone that can help with that—my friend Charles Logan."

The committee shook their heads and the conversation turned to the legal ramifications for the retirement home if a resident gets out and is subsequently liable in a court of law. The director appeared in the doorway soon after the lawsuit was mentioned and squashed any liability concerns for all those in attendance other than Archie, who was now pacing from wall to wall behind his father's chair. When they got back to the burden of Alton, the committee agreed it was lucky there was a perfectly acceptable, state-approved locked unit on the premises. The rate would be higher, but the doors locked from the outside and Archie was assured Medicare would pay for most of the stay.

"We'll do private pay for the time being, until the papers are sorted out," Murray said to the room. "So we can get him into the wing this evening."

"Did you feed the cows?" was thumping through his head with each heartbeat.

His senses heightened and he drank in the room around him as a collision of sensibilities. He smelled the cologne of someone in the room—it smelled like a well-oiled saddle. He felt Archie's feet stomping behind him, hitting the carpet and moving the rotting boards beneath. He thought he might pluck the wings clean off a passing mosquito with this focus. He heard the faint grumble of a busied state employee behind him, somewhere standing in thick heels on the thin carpet. The hollow thud of a finger hitting a WriteWayz E-Pad played like a dull orchestral number. He wondered what she thought of him. Did the catch impress her? Did she see it?

"If you've nothing to add," Gunnar said, standing in a moment and flattening his khaki pants, "it seems the matter settled, and we can call it a night, huh, fellas?"

The others sitting behind the white, plastic, folding tables began to stand, the sound of leveraging against the table joints echoed about the room as they pressed down to stand up.

"Do you mean me?" Tapscott asked. The room seemed to stop. "Do I have something to say?"

"Well, sure, Mr. Tapscott," Gunnar said, nodding, glancing to his dad.

Cooper lifted a hand and motioned for the committee members to remain in place.

"Your son is technically your responsible party, but you can certainly let us know if there's something you need or want in your new wing." He was wrapping a navy blazer around broad shoulder, sweeping the jacket around in the air, his back turned to the room.

"If this is my life's resignation letter," Alton said, "then I wouldn't mind authoring it myself, you see?" He tilted his head a bit and smiled. The committee continued to pack their bags and stretch their joints as he settled into his speech. "The man that came in is not the man going out, and at least I can say I tried.

"For too long, I was consumed by any idea contrary to the present. Any movie that predicts a bleak future will eventually hit its mark, but that doesn't mean life isn't worth living before we fuck it all up, right? Gas prices are too high, the Earth is melting, kids don't mind, and politicians are liars … but hasn't that always been the case?" He pressed his palms into the plush arms of the red chair and stood balancing as each leg muscle locked into position, turning on a heel and craning his neck to see Archie in the corner of the room. "And for that, I apologize, Archer. I let you down."

Archie flashed a soft smile and nodded.

"And yeah, I got out. Let us give no more scrutiny to this event or those of the stadium—a bawdy den of perverts loyal to a mediocre program. And if I apologize maybe that'll make things better, but maybe I'm just not that good of a guy. I just wanted to chase what's left of life. Is it too much to seek the existence of the lower middle class for a morning of baseball? Which of you palate-less sheep hasn't chased the price of a mid-sized Volkswagen to appease your wife? Sacrificed your taste and decency for the J & D Power safety rating? You'll all be scuttled into the depths of history like this one day, too … no permanent mark left on society. Ask yourself how I got here? I just wanted to enjoy what was left. I've been living my life cruising through greens, and I've been speeding through a yellow light since I got here, trying to make the most of it but it's too late. Maybe it's enlightenment enough to know I'm always changing, no smug clarity at the end. Maybe, for me, life's just about realizing how small I am, and stubborn, and how far I have left to go. I just wanted to enjoy, to enjoy—"

Just then, he felt someone standing behind him, so close he moved his shoulder as if a phantom pushed him. It was Ms.

Ledbetter, the woman in the gray suit, not looking up but moving forward, step by step, toward the tables. The room sat still. He attempted to gather his mind, the thumping on the WriteWayz E-pad like a bass drum in unison with his heartbeat. She stopped to adjust a rogue strand of hair. The room paused for a moment, just Alton Tapscott and a woman in a stark gray suit standing in the middle.

"Oh! Oh my gaw-sh," she said, backing away. "I apologize, Mr. Tap. Mr. Scott. Tapscott. I am so sorry. Is that Scottish? I didn't meanta interrupt. You were saying …"

He looked back to the committee, their eyes darting to him, then her. He shrugged a bit, then looked into her gray eyes which felt warmer than before. He noticed she was smiling and realized it might be the first real smile he received in a long time. "I don't quite remember where I was headed," he said.

"Something about you being not a good person?" she said, looking down to the pad and giving a cursory shrug.

"Oh, yes, well, I was going to use that to lead into my next point which starts with a Thoreau quote from my journey to the outdoors today. Something about the great outdoors, baseball, America's game, I am America—" He stopped, letting the thought continue adrift in his head.

"Actually," Ms. Ledbetter said, taking a quick jump-step forward, "if I may, this might be the perfect time to clear up some questions I was havin'."

A committee member asked if the questions revolved around tonight's proceedings, which she said no. The director asked if she'd like to step into his office, which she declined. Tapscott asked if it was about his catch that day, which she assured him it was not.

"I wanted to bring the, um," she paused, swiping her finger on the pad's screen, scrolling as the glow of the pad made her sharp eyebrows thicken, "the Living and Orifice Debris Dis-in-fect-or-i-zor, Disinfectorizor, the L.O.D.D., the Elodie, back in. Is that okay?"

The director assured her anything she was looking for they would produce—there was nothing to hide. Marlon rolled Elodie back into the clubhouse den on the food cart and pulled back the steamer top, revealing the same hexagonal robot E.B. unwrapped in the apartment weeks before.

"How do I play back the audio?" Ms. Ledbetter asked. "I'd love to hear that bit again about the comptroller. The Parish comptroller. He's babbling about something, and it got cut off," she talked as she peered into the monitor screen atop Elodie's black shell. She punched it with her index finger before a menu came up and she motioned for the director to come deal with it.

There again was his voice, still a bit shrill, going on about the Parish comptroller. Still confident and yet unsure. Then the unzipping, then the trickle of water works, and then again Tapscott was thankful when the director stepped in to stop the audio.

"Do we need to listen to a man urinate?" he asked. His plaid blue shirt became untucked throughout the proceedings, and he now stood a frazzled mess, hair coming undone, parts of his body indiscriminately wet. He was still smiling.

"No, this is it," she said, her hand resting on the time of the recording, while the other plugged the time it into her pad. "Play this part."

The audio started again, the pace of the droplets splashing on the water's surface picked up, gaining momentum until a mature stream came through. Tapscott nodded proudly, surveying the room. Take away the impending locked unit and blast off pills, and this day was shaping up to be a real self-esteem boost. A muffled voice on the recording cursed as the stream broke for a second, then the sounds of the droll patter of liquid on a porcelain toilet seat, then it sounded like splatters on linoleum floor. Then a sharp yelp burst from Elodie followed by the squeaking of slippery feet and the thud of a human torso hitting the tile. The trickling sound of a leaky faucet continued for a moment until Tapscott's voice came through again, complaining of the small confines of the bathroom.

"That dumb ass walker salesman. That fiend. That idiot sold me the biggest walker on the market, and it won't even fit in the bathroom."

The audio continued as Ms. Ledbetter nodded and pointed her finger at the robot as if to say "that's it," punching in something on her pad. Tapscott sensed his eye twitching, and a tinge of remorse came over him—he didn't know he'd degraded his walker, and he needed it now more than ever as he stood alone in this stuffy room. He glanced at the off-white crown molding around the room and felt it was either closing in or losing its glue.

"He fell," Cooper Murray interjected, walking toward the food cart. "We noted that in our report to your office. I filled out the report myself, Ms. Ledbetter."

"*You* did," she said, not looking up from her pad. "You did indeed. But, if I may, you are a resident here. You do not work here, and so—"

"Well, no," Murray shot back, "I'm not an employee, but I do serve as the direct resident liaison to the director, and, as Resident Council President, I am allotted certain clerical rights over the residents I serve."

Ms. Ledbetter looked confused. She motioned for the director who scurried over to the group huddled near the food cart. Elodie was still playing the recording, which moved on to

Tapscott trying to stand up and shower, slipping multiple times and yelling out again.

"So," she started after filing through some papers, "my thing is, I want what's best for everyone, but I have to go by the forms the state gives me. And, according to the form now, a resident of that size, with that sized walking assistance apparatus, should only be housed in an apartment with a bathroom that included an eight-foot birth from wall-to-wall, measuring floor-to-floor within one foot of the threshold. And," she pulled a piece of paper out with a scribbled note on top, "I measured the bathrooms today, and Mr. Tapscott's apartment's bathroom is only a seven-foot birth. He's a walkie-talkie, is he not?"

The director looked puzzled. He took the paper from her and studied the measurements on the note.

"Listen, I hate to do this, but I really have no choice … it's what's in the form," she said.

"What are we supposed to do," Murray asked, "break down a wall? He needed a room and that's all we had. He wasn't a walkie-talkie all the time!"

The woman's eyes softened as her head tilted, and a small, gentle smile appeared. "It's not your fault," she stopped for a moment to study a sheet of paper on her clipboard, "Mr. Cooper. You're not the director."

"But I am the Resident Council President and the liaison to the director!" he said.

Tapscott took a step back, and he saw Ms. Ledbetter's expression harden as her voice lowered.

"Now, sir, I am going to have to ask that you calm down."

"I am plenty calm," Cooper Murray said as eyes in the room fell on him. "I have been running this place since I got here, and you're … you're going to tell me it's not up to code?" He threw his arms wide, gesturing to the expanse of the den. "What do you know about keeping these people in line? You're clearly not from the city anyway. You don't even work *in* a nursing home!"

Her gray suit stiffened, heels dug into the green, syrup-drenched carpet. "Neither do you, Mr. Cooper, and it's a retirement community, not approved for Medicare funds, either, I might add." Then without pause, she burst into what sounded to Tapscott like either a military drill or religious trance. "According to the bylaws agreed upon by this facility's *board of trustees* with the State of Louisiana, a resident of that size, with that size walking assistance appar-atus, should only be housed in an apartment with a bathroom that includes an eight-foot birth from wall-to-wall, measuring floor-to-floor within one foot of the threshold." She stared at Murray for a moment before turning on the director. "I will need a list of all residents, their weights, their self-transportation ability scores, and a floor plan. I would suggest selecting the residents' quarters yourself from now on and not letting them run themselves. After I complete my investigation, I will let you know how many penalties you've incurred, but we are at least up to one now. No more resident-initiated disciplinary hearings either, that's for the licensed professionals in the room."

She gathered her things and sped out of the room leaving a trail of open, dry-mouthed men. She only stopped to ask Alton if he understood what was going on. He flashed a naive puppy grin and nodded. She hugged him, and her heels clanked down the wooden hall. Nobody said a word until the squeaking hinges of the front double-doors slammed shut. Tapscott clapped twice before the echo hit him in the silent room.

"Well, now," Cooper Murray said, shaking his head with a smile, "she was sumthin, huh?"

The room stayed quiet.

"Look, we'll get this straightened out, but as for all this today and tonight—"

The director held up a hand. He was staring down at the ground. "This carpet is disgusting," he said. "How did it get this way?"

Cooper looked around. "I'll have Marlon clean it in the morning—"

"No," the director said with a long sigh. "No. Cooper, you've been a real presence up here for so long. You're a valued member of our community for sure, for sure. I … I just think it might be time to enjoy your retirement. Ya know?"

Cooper Murray's face was as red as the embroidered sailing flag on his belt. "No, I don't know. Gunnar? Help out here. This is ridiculous. Gunnar?"

Tapscott turned to see Gunnar Murray sitting down at the folding table again. His elbows were up on the surface, and the glow of his phone screen gleamed on his face.

He shook his head then rose with his eyes closed as if he'd been asleep.

"Sorry, Dad." Gunnar looked down at his phone again for a brief second, smiled, then looked back to Cooper. "What's goin' on now? I had something come up at … work … and need to skedaddle soon. Is this all over?"

Murray tried explaining the situation to his son, but the director and Gunnar agreed the night was getting away from them and it was time for supper. Tapscott offered to resume his speech, but the room agreed it wasn't important anymore. The director offered Cooper the chance to resign from his role as Resident Council President and resident liaison to the director. He told Cooper to run again in the fall and see how it went, but Cooper declined, ripping off the "P" from his St. Ignatius

"President" jacket lapel, and tossing it on the ground at Gunnar and the director's feet. They asked E.B. to escort Cooper Murray back to his room. Tapscott locked eyes with Cooper as E.B. grasped his arm, cupping Cooper's elbow and leading him by the wrist. Cooper Murray's blank expression ranging from his wrist to Tapscott like he was trying to spot the difference. When he finally walked out, pausing every few steps and to look back over his shoulder at the men in the room, his son was mimicking his golf swing for the rest of the Elderly Ethics Committee.

Tapscott went to speak, to give a comforting smile or nod, but he knew it would only be false. Besides, he quite respected the indecency of the moment and wanted Cooper to realize his own path, his own haunting reaction to resentment that Tapscott could still feel in his bones. As for himself, he was standing in the middle of the room and no amount of excitement could keep him vertical for much longer.

Marlon was at the door of the clubhouse, motioning for Tapscott to come his way. He had the Simpson's cabernet red, medical-grade, deluxe, two-button, folding, aluminum walker in the hallway. Tapscott fell into it like a warm bath.

*****

He returned to the courtyard that night a conquistador. Noel Cone greeted him with a bone-crunching hug, others with back pats, Zach Majoria with some pizza they'd ordered, and Cricket Kirby with the Psalm she'd read while he was in there. He told them everything, each moment getting a larger gasp. Poppy Burt was sure Ms. Ledbetter was up to something and cursed her L.O.D.D. when she heard they recorded residents.

"Poor Cooper."

They all smiled.

"Drives that son of his crazy, I'm sure," Deacon Kirby said. "But don't we all?"

"Not Tapscott," he assured them.

Archie saw Alton back to the door, but the two didn't speak. Tapscott planned to call his friend and attorney, Charles Logan, in the morning to transfer the rest of his will to the Zippy's Mexican Cantina delivery boy, along with the German-engineered sandals, in a spiteful legal sneak attack that he hoped would get a more spirited Archie back on the phone. He didn't have much except for an old solar-powered Subaru, some cat supplies, and a chair.

It wasn't long before Marlon came running down again with Elodie tucked under his arm, which made Poppy stay quiet for a few minutes until the robot rolled inside. Tapscott dusted her off, glad to see her out of that dining cart. The group sat in the warm summer heat, the swirling winds of a mild tropical event picking up on the treetops before a light shower sent them scattering to their respective porches. They yelled goodnight through a dense rain, Tapscott lingering a minute longer to hear the doors shut behind.

He went into his apartment later on, drenched but buoyant with possibility, to see his belongings half-packed, like a burglar caught with the lights on. The lamp in the corner flickered as he plopped onto his green chair, its musty cloth felt cold but comfortable on his face. He surveyed the apartment, virtually untouched since his arrival, his impact a few cardboard packing boxes away from utter annihilation. A bulletin with next week's activities was standing on the coffee table next to the chair and he saw from the cover it was the same as the previous few— Chinese New Year was coming up again, two times next week, and creamed corn was back in season. He sat, mugged by the reality of his future and circumstance.

His guts started to churn, and his skin went cold where the raindrops sat on his arms and neck. He'd never experienced a diabetic shock before but was always on the lookout for weight-related incidents. He scarfed down a bowl of cheese dip that afternoon thinking it might be his last, so maybe it was the block of fluorescent yellow cheese-flavored product and canned tomatoes, the pizza he just ate, or perhaps the idea swirling about his head that despite a day of considerable personal victory, he was still resigned to this room and this place, no Mack in sight and no more family to falsely lean on. It was just him now, so he saw it. The thought of Noel warmed him for a moment, as the idea of friends often did, but the darkness of the room closed in and a throbbing sensation gripped his ear. His life was undeniably mostly done for, his best years sent off like a Viking funeral with paltry attendance or circumstance.

"I stood up for myself today, LIZA … and look where it got me!" A soft blue light flickered in the dull room as LIZA registered his statement.

"*Should I share your location, Mister Tapscott?*"

His head felt light, dizzy again with either excitement or fear, and his right eye twitched. He sneezed twice in succession and felt a sharp pain in his abdomen, which he grabbed, the skin beneath his white robe burning. In the back of his mind, his father's often-recited warning came to him. "Don't go living your life fat, bald, and dumb. Wouldn't want to waste my sperm on that."

He wasn't completely bald yet.

"LIZA, can you hear me?" he whispered as he winced. "What are the symptoms of dying?"

"*I don't know, Mister Tapscott, I've never died.*"

"Of course, you haven't," he said, breaths paced, sipping air through his dried lips between each word, his body slinking out of the chair and onto the floor. "But look it up then, will you?" He held his teeth, gritting and grinding with his eyes closed tight.

"*They say you see your loved ones, your friends, relatives, old pets, and visiting angels—the ones that've died before you—and they embrace you. They say it's a dreamlike state and you feel a deep peace, a comforting presence, and you are not afraid. They say those that will miss you feel a tinge of acceptance and you feel welcomed to a better place. They say it is warm, and it is perfect.*"

He winced again. "At least I went out with a bang. Not every life is this well lived, LIZA. Every drop … drank."

"*Yes, they do also say people become rather narcissistic around death.*"

His stomach boiling, a sensation climbed his esophagus like a scalding corkscrew.

He burped.

"Oh, damn," he said, exhaling as through a whale's blowhole. "Probably just bad gas then." He opened his eyes. "LIZA, I'm sure you heard all the hullabaloo about my TV segment today?"

Tapscott sat up, pulling on the coffee table and chair until he could lean against the wall. His eyes darted toward the front as a muted, frantic scratch beat against his apartment's aluminum door. A flash of teal swept by the partially opened blinds, the rain falling in rhythm to the ceaseless drum.

ACKNOWLEDGEMENTS

Two people made this book a foreseeable possibility—Malise and Dennis O'Banion. My dad likes to mention divinely gifted athletes or particularly wealthy descendants as being given a "lucky sperm award," and I consider myself in that group. My mom has always encouraged and supported my writing—even gifting me a novel to "read when I was bored" after getting into law school. Thank you, mom and dad.

I owe an extraordinary debt to my wife, Melissa, for gifting me time and patience while she worked a real job and raised a real family. When I presented the idea of pursuing an MFA and a book deal, she was either too busy or too trusting to put up much of a fight. Thank you.

I would also like to acknowledge my kids, Flannery and Henry. Henry was sitting next to me recently, I thought watching me type and hoping he was impressed with either my home row key strategy or speed. He must've gotten bored and crawled on the bed where he and Flannery growled and snarled back and forth before grabbing my collar and pulling me onto a guest bed duvet covered in dog and cat hair, facing a TV without a remote. They snarled and growled, "I'm gonna eat you up," and I love them in the exact same way.

Many friends shaped characters in this story and have shaped my life in various ways, and I'd be remiss if I didn't mention Jarrod Cone and Ryan Tapscott from the outset. Jarrod being my closest friend and Ryan being my greatest confusion. I love them both. I would also like to thank other friends that have supported, shaped, or taken interest in my work along the way: Corey, Mitchel, Preston, Clay B., Edward, Nick, Taylor, Doug, Tripp, Haltzman, Bryce, TJ, Joe, Dave, Chase, Josh, and Doran; and a disturbing amount of Shreveport natives: Noah, Baynham, Cobb, Ross, Allie, and Seth.

My siblings, all older and lighter, have always been an exceptional example and destination on a human level. Thank you, Katie, David, Leigh, and Mary Claire.

I want to mention the work of two authors and mentors that without whom this book would either not exist: Victoria Patterson and Jim Krusoe. Thank you for taking an interest in me and my work.

Other authors I admire and strive to read more of include Shalom Auslander, Jeanne Leiby, John Kennedy Toole, Kurt Vonnegut, Tomas Moniz, Flannery O'Connor, Karen Gaul-Schulman, James Wilcox, Ahsan Butt, Dan O'Brien, Douglas Adams, F. Scott Fitzgerald, David Foster Wallace, Roger Kahn, Franz Kafka, William Golding, Antoine de Saint-Exupéry, David Sedaris, M.O. Walsh, Amy Hempel, Flann O'Brien, Roberto Bolano, Fredick Backman, and Ken Kesey. Some, like Toole, O'Connor, and Vonnegut, showed me what was possible in fiction while others like Gaul-Schulman and Butt showed me great passion and purpose. Jeanne Leiby gave me my first opportunity to edit and think on a literary level at the Southern Review Literary Journal, and I miss her guidance. And a special note of appreciation to Matthew Blasi and Brooke Parsons for editing and advice that got me to this point.

A special thanks to John B. Mclemore and Brian Reed for the podcast S*Town, which I drew inspiration and words from on multiple occasions—a redneck Frasier—which is what this could have been if based in Alabama. And thank you to Joe Burrow, Daniel Dumile, Wes Anderson, and other cultural figures—I enjoy your work.

My friend Kim Howard (@kimwimble) created the map on page 31and Brian Callaghan created the cover art as well as some incredible baseball images that he releases on his Instagram (@hokiecal_art).

And finally, Dino Price, the publisher and one of many editors on this book, has my sincere and perpetual gratitude. Mr. Price took a chance on me and gave me his time, expertise, and ear. He was exceedingly patient and helpful throughout and has made this process a bearable pleasure. Thank you, Dino.

About C.E. O'Banion

C.E. O'Banion is a father of two and writer based in Baton Rouge, LA. He writes about his generation, his family, his hometown, and his favorite chain Mexican restaurants. His short stories and essays have previously appeared online and in print in The Southern Review, The Deal Mule, Mouthing Off Magazine, Whalebone Magainze, Short Beasts, and others. He is also an editor of Two Hawks Quarterly out of Antioch University (Los Angeles).

Chinese New Year is his debut novel, and he has also completed a collection of short stories about his upbringing in East Texas. His short nonfiction was nominated for a Pushcart Prize in 2022.

O'Banion graduated from Louisiana State University with a Bachelor's in English and later a Juris Doctorate. He has an MFA degree in creative writing from Antioch University in Los Angeles in conjunction with the USC Writer's Workshop. O'Banion has worked as an editor, welder, attorney, teacher, cake decorator, lobbyist, and nursing home administrator, where he was made to celebrate Chinese New Year monthly.

O'Banion and his wife, Melissa, have been married for seven years and have two children, Flannery and Henry. They also have a dog, Joan of Bark, and a cat, EZ Mac. He can be found through his agent at www.ceobanion.com and welcomes emails and messages from readers.

CPSIA information can be obtained
at www.ICGtesting.com
Printed in the USA
BVHW051232230323
661006BV00015B/783